AN ALLIANCE FOR NIKOLAI

NIKOLAI

ANN CAROLL

Book cover by Ann Caroll

Proofreading by Kate Wood

Trigger Warnings

This book does feature dark, mature themes. Including:

- Stalking (not by MMC)

- Violence (i.e., torture, weapons, blood)

- Drug addiction of parent (mentioned)

- Alcoholism of a parent (mentioned)

- Childhood trauma & abuse

- Murder

- Rough, kinky sex (including light D/s dynamics)

This book may not be for everyone. That is okay. Please prioritize your mental health and well-being if any of these themes may trigger you.

FEDOROV FAMILY

Mikhail Fedorov: *(Misha)* Pakhan of Fedorov Bratva. Husband to Sierra. Father of Tatiana & Alexandra.

Sierra Fedorov: Wife of Misha and stepmother to Tatiana & Alexandra. Nurse for Fedorov Bratva.

Tatiana Fedorov: *(Tati)* Daughter of Misha, stepdaughter to Sierra. Older sister of Alexandra. Current heir to Fedorov Bratva.

Alexandra Fedorov: Daughter of Misha, stepdaughter to Sierra. Younger sister of Tatiana.

Anatoly Fedorov: *(Toly)* 2nd-in-command for his older brother. Also heads intelligence & surveillance for the Bratva.

Nikolai Fedorov: *(Niko)* Youngest of Fedorov brothers. Is the Bratva's accountant.

Vladimir Fedorov: *(Vlad)* 1st cousin of Misha, Toly, & Niko Fedorov. Is the head enforcer for the Bratva. Older brother of Dimitri.

Dimitri Fedorov: *(Dima)* 1st cousin of Misha, Toly, & Niko Fedorov. Is the doctor & occasional sniper for the Bratva. Younger brother of Vladimir.

Maxim & Anastasia Fedorov: Parents to Misha, Toly, & Niko. Uncle and aunt to Vlad & Dima. Maxim retired from being Pakhan 15 years prior. Both are alive and split time between Chicago & Moscow.

To the people who found their peace and have a partner who is willing to do anything for them to keep it.

BLURB

With a special birthday goal, Mariah Perez and Nikolai Fedorov maintain a secret contract where he aims to teach her everything there is to enjoy about sex. As Mariah starts getting mysterious phone calls and the feeling that she's being followed, and receives threatening letters, Nikolai vows to protect her at all costs.

Mariah has spent her whole life avoiding men and relationships. She discovers new familial connections that change her life forever. She looks to Nikolai for more than just protection as she navigates a new reality while staying safe from danger lurking in the shadows.

*While this is a stand-alone book within a series, it is best read after *A Nanny For Mikhail*. Certain characters and storylines carry over and reading book 1 will provide additional context.

TABLE OF CONTENTS

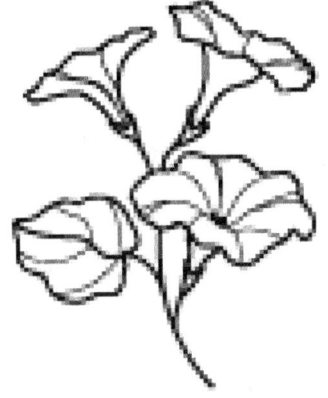

CHAPTER 1

NIKO

I 've been in love with a woman for nearly six months, and she has no idea. Mariah Perez has had me captivated since the moment I met her. I've spent my entire thirty years on this planet avoiding attachments to people outside of my family and my best friend, but Mariah has broken through those walls somehow. Well, okay I know how she did it. She's stunningly beautiful, with dark brown eyes and wavy hair the color of honey. She is tough, but I can tell there's more to her than she lets anyone else see, even her best friend and my new sister-in-law, Sierra.

Mariah has no idea how I feel about her, and likely, it'll stay that way, because I know how she feels regarding relationships. She's extremely shy around men, almost wary. But if I ever got the slightest hint that she'd be ready for more, I would be all in before she could change her mind.

We met six months ago when my brother, Anatoly, and I told our older brother Mikhail to get a nanny. That nanny ended up being Sierra, our new sister-in-law, who's pregnant with our newest niece or nephew. She started to bring her best friend and roommate, Mariah, around after she started working for my brother. I remember everything about the day I met her.

Six Months Ago: Early June

Taking my dog Rasputin for a walk, I check my phone and see a text message from my cousin, Vladimir, asking if I can cover him tomorrow. He needs help guarding our nieces and their new nanny when they go to the Art Institute. I let him know that I can cover, and I'll be at Misha's to keep them safe.

The next morning, I pull into my brother's driveway and the young soldier, Ilya, lets me through the gates. I meet the other guards who'll be coming with us, and I start to prep the SUVs for the girls. As I grab another set of keys from the hook in the foyer, my nieces come barreling down the stairs. Tati and Alexandra give me hugs and run out the front door, excited for their day at the museum. I follow them outside. Hearing the front door shut again, I turn around to see who came out behind us and I see Sierra, the new nanny, but next to her is a shorter woman. She's fucking beautiful. When Sierra introduces us, I learn her name is Mariah. Her smile is kind and her eyes draw me in further.

I open the car door for her and get a whiff of her perfume. She smells like rose and vanilla. The scent floods my nostrils, and I know I'll never forget this scent for the rest of my life. As we drive to the museum, I keep checking the rearview mirror to get additional glances at Mariah without her noticing. Silently, I'm chastising myself because I've never been drawn to a woman like this. She's bewitched me by just saying hello, and just being near me. I've got to cool it, otherwise she's going to think I'm a complete psycho.

We spend the rest of the afternoon walking around the museum. I know how much Alexandra loves to be around art, so she's fully in her element. Mariah is helping keep my older niece, Tati, occupied so that her teenage antics don't keep Alexandra from having a great time. After we get back to the house and drop the girls off, I head over to my BDSM club, Rapture, which I opened a couple years ago. I'm here for my scheduled weekly meeting with my sub. She's doing fine as a submissive, but it's been almost four months. I normally don't keep a contract for this long. I usually stick to three months. She maintains the boundaries I've set, but as soon as I walk through the front door tonight, I'm distracted and not in the right headspace. All I can think about is Mariah, and how good she'd feel in my arms, under me, and on top of me. *Fuck.* Having her ride me could send me into an early grave.

I send my sub away and apologize for my lack of interest in doing a scene right now. I end up leaving less than thirty minutes after I arrive, and once I'm back in the comfort of my penthouse, I text my sub. I break our contract and let her know that she was amazing, but my head isn't in it right now to maintain that relationship. She's cordial and maintains the boundaries outlined in our original contract. I'm grateful that it didn't get messy.

Ever since that night, I have spent my time alone and celibate, despite owning a sex club, because I can't get this woman out of my head. My secret crush is made worse a month later.

Five Months Ago: Late July

I'm sitting in my office when I hear my brother, Misha, yelling that we need to go. He's screaming for help. I run to him and see that he's currently hauling ass to a car. I follow and jump into the passenger seat. Over the Bluetooth speaker, I hear Mariah's voice. She's breathing hard and crying. I hear her say that she's scared. I clench my jaw to avoid speaking and taking over this call. I need to get to her. I need to save her.

Misha asks her where she's at.

"I don't know, I'm running north from the salon." Mariah is panicking.

"Try to stay calm, okay? We're coming for you." Misha tries to talk her down a bit.

When we get there, we start to search the alley for them. From behind a dumpster, Mariah reveals herself and she's carrying my ten-year-old niece, Alexandra. Mariah is a short woman, so when she's carrying Alexandra who's maybe only four inches shorter than her, it's a feat. I give them both a look over and that's when I see Mariah's bloody feet and deep cuts.

I quickly jump into action as Misha takes Alexandra from Mariah's arms. I gather the woman who's been on my mind constantly for the past month into my arms. I start to whisper in her ear my thanks for saving Alexandra. "Mariah, I promise, I'll get you help. I'll take care of you."

She just leans her head into my chest. I hold her the entire way back to my brother's house. I run her down to my cousin, Dima, our Bratva's doctor, so he can look at her feet. He spends the better part of an hour cleaning them and getting glass and debris out of the dozens of cuts.

Dima tells her, "Mariah, please try to stay off your feet whenever you can over the next week or so, but especially tonight."

I quickly answer him. "I'll make sure she's taken care of."

I look at her, and she gratefully nods at my overbearing attempts to help. She has to know by now, especially after the past few weeks, that I'm down bad for her. I've been able to tell that she's shy around men. She avoids eye contact with our guards, and I know Sierra's said she doesn't date. I don't know why that is, but I'm willing to play the long game with Mariah. I want her, and I've spent the last month thinking about her constantly.

"I'm going to help you tonight, okay?"

She nods. "Thank you, Niko, I don't want to bother any of you, though. You need to find Sierra."

"I promise, the entire family is looking for her. Let's get you upstairs. I know Irina would love to coddle someone right now, and I think you're the lucky winner." She gives me a small laugh.

I carry her up the stairs to the living room. Gently, I prop her feet up once I've set her down on the couch. Even though I want to spend time taking care of her, I also need to help my family find Sierra and our cousin, Vlad. "I'll find Irina and send her in here, but I have to go check in with Misha to see if he's learned anything so far, okay?" She nods and smiles gratefully. I find Irina in the kitchen, and I ask her to check in on Mariah while I meet with the family.

"Of course, Niko. I'll make sure she has everything she needs. I heard she saved Alexandra today. Are her injuries bad?"

"She did, she got her out of there and kept her from Sergei. She's a hero today. And she's got some pretty gnarly cuts on the bottoms of her feet, but overall she'll be okay."

I go in search of my brothers, finding them in the conference room. I sit with them for a while to help find our missing people. Misha asks if he can talk to Mariah, so I walk with him to the living room where Irina is currently tending to her feet by changing the ice packs that Dima had wrapped around them downstairs in the clinic. We ask her for a total rundown of everything. As she finishes recounting what happened, she starts to cry again. Her tears wreck me. I never had sisters growing up, but having helped raise my nieces after Misha's wife Elena passed away, I've gotten used to tears. However, I don't think I'll ever be able to get used to seeing her upset. I sit next to her on the couch and hold her hand. "It's okay, Mariah, you did everything right," I reassure her.

After my brother goes back to the office wing in his house, I continue to sit with Mariah. I call Sam Aslanov, my best friend. He works with my family, but in our legitimate businesses. He's the CFO of Fedorov Industries but is someone who was raised in this life. His father worked for mine, so we grew up together. We were roommates in college, both of us going to NYU for accounting.

Over the past few weeks, he's been helping direct my team to scour real estate transactions, hoping to find something that matches a withdrawal Sergei Kuznetsov made a few weeks back. We're currently at war with Misha's former father-in-law, and now he's kidnapped Sierra and Vlad.

I run my hand through Mariah's hair as she tries to sleep after an adrenaline crash. "Would you come to my penthouse after this is over so I can help you? I don't want you to be alone, and Misha won't let Sierra out of his sight."

"I don't want to be an inconvenience, Niko."

"You're never an inconvenience. I want to help you." She must see that I'm being genuine and agrees to let me take care of her.

A few hours later, a text comes through on the group chat with my brothers and cousins.

> Misha: We have a location. Leaving in five minutes.

> On my way.

After the rescue mission, we're back at the house with both Sierra and Vlad. Our brother has his woman back and we have our cousin back, too. Sergei and Nikita are both dead, meaning the threat to our nieces has been neutralized.

After Mariah has gotten to hug Sierra, I carry her out to my car to drive her to my penthouse. Once the private elevator lands on my floor, I open the door. There's only one other penthouse located on this floor and it's owned by my brother, Toly. It makes it easy for the guards on staff here to protect us. Walking into my home, I carry her to a guest room and offer her a t-shirt to change into, and she nods, but I can tell she wants to take a shower. Unfortunately, with her injured feet, she's not going to be able to stand.

"Would you want to use my bathroom? I have a tub that also has a movable faucet, so you'll be able to keep your feet dry."

"That'd be amazing. I feel so gross and I just want to wash off this day," she responds meekly.

Logistically, I know that she'll be too nervous to let me help her into the bath if she's naked. She's only in a t-shirt and shorts, so she should be okay to slide off her clothes without needing help. Helping her into the tub, I instruct her on how to use the faucet. I also set a big towel down next to the tub for when she's done.

"Let me know when you're done and I'll help you get back to the guest room. Would you like something to eat? I was thinking of just making some sandwiches."

"I'm not picky, so a sandwich would be good. Thank you for your help, Niko. I'm sure you have other things you could be doing."

If only she knew that taking care of her is all I want to do tonight.

"No, I want to help you. Enjoy your bath. I'll get some food together."

She takes her time in the tub before calling me to help her get out. I walk in, and she was able to secure the towel around her body, so I carefully pick her up and bring her to the guest room. She's able to put on the t-shirt and boxers that I laid out for her.

We end up eating a late dinner together and spending a few hours talking. She opens up to me, and I learn so much about her.

She tells me about her childhood, how bad things were with her mom. The abuse she suffered at the hands of her mom is terrible. No child should ever face that. She shares with me that she recently took a DNA test, and just got the results back. She found out that she's got a paternal half brother. I can tell she's nervous to reach out, so I offer my assistance, "If there's anything I can do to help, let me know."

"Thanks, Niko. I'm not even sure I'll reach out to him, but we'll see."

***

From that night on, I continue to lay the groundwork slowly. After learning about how her mother had sketchy men over to their house regularly, and the verbal abuse, and neglect she suffered, I understand better why she is so hesitant around men.

I know that Mariah is different from any other woman I've ever been with. Normally, I keep my interactions with women to the confines of Rapture. A contract is involved, and there are clear boundaries. We have prior discussions on what is in play and what is a hard no. With Mariah, I want what my brother has with Sierra. I want more than what I've had before, which scares the shit out of me. I don't want to fail, because deep down, I know that I've only got one shot with her.

She's alluded to not being interested in relationships, and Sierra's hinted at that when she's caught me flirting. At this point, I'll take Mariah however I can get her, but I know she's it for me.

Sitting in my office with Sam, going over reports, I notice that he's still nervous around Tati when she's with us in a work capacity. She started her training with me just a couple of weeks ago, after spending nearly a year learning surveillance and hacking from my brother, Toly. Sam's not upset that our family will be led by Tati one day, I think he's just nervous to tell her something that will shock her. I've told him a few times that she's seen things, even gone on missions. Her first being Sierra and Vlad's rescue back in July.

I also think that he doesn't want to put her in awkward positions with the financials. Even though Sam deals with our legitimate business, he does help occasionally with our money laundering when things get busy.

"Uncle Niko, if we do inventory at the bars and clubs every other week, is there a way that we could do it electronically? Having the managers all go through by hand and sending them to the offices with a soldier seems prehistoric," Tati comments.

Sam turns his head to the comfy dark blue couch that sits up against the wall of my office. She's sitting with her legs folded and laptop balancing on the armrest. Addressing her question directly, my friend answers, "I know what you mean. It's a good idea, Tati. We just haven't made it a priority, but as time has gone on, I agree that it's become more cumbersome to maintain doing it by hand. Not just because it's ancient, but because of the additional liquors and kegs we carry."

"I get that. Those parts of our business are legitimate, right?"

I respond to my niece. "Yes, that's correct. This is just run-of-the-mill inventory; would you want to make that a project to work on modernizing?"

"Yeah, I could try. Maybe figuring out a way to have each manager use a tablet that can be uploaded directly to a Fedorov server so we can get real-time data? I bet we can even have sales set up to the same server to help streamline doing the books at all legitimate businesses."

"That's a good place to start. It'd definitely cut down on hounding staff to send in reports on time." Sam laughs.

I turn to look at my niece, who happily is taking on a project that will directly help our businesses. I'm really proud of how hard she's working to learn about leading the Bratva.

Moving on, we show Tati how the cash flow at the strip clubs can be manipulated to flush dirty cash through to make it clean. She's intrigued, and asks questions that even Sam is impressed by.

"What is this column over here, Sam?" Tati asks as she points to my friend's laptop screen.

"That's the community fund. We set this up at every business. We take a percentage from the profits and put it back into the community. It funds things like soup kitchens, domestic violence shelters, and even school lunches. That all gets paid from this line item."

"Is that something we've always done?"

Sam looks at me to answer this question, because he knows the answer is a tough one. "No. Actually, it was your mom's idea after she married your dad. She thought it would help with our image, but also provide for the communities we help protect."

Tati smiles when she hears that it was her mom's idea. Elena, her mom and Misha's first wife, really was a born and raised Bratva wife. She was formidable, and with her by my brother's side, he was able to successfully assume power from our father when he retired.

Her death rocked our entire family. Even though their marriage was arranged, I know Misha loved her as the mother of his daughters. She was my sister in every way that mattered. I'm glad that we now have Sierra, who, like the rest of us, is determined to keep Elena's memory alive for Tati and Alexandra.

We wrap up walking Tati through reports to finish our meeting so she can go with Misha and Sierra to their doctor's appointment.

Today, we're finding out the gender of their baby. To make them feel included, Sierra is having Tati and Alexandra throw a gender reveal party during dinner. Tati stands to leave and gives me a hug, and I kiss the top of her head. She quickly gives Sam a hug too before heading out.

After she leaves my office, Sam and I settle back into working. He brings up some crypto opportunities that could be lucrative. I bring up some topics covering our estate portfolio, including the sale of a warehouse on the south side to the Alvarez Cartel.

"Will I see you at Rapture tonight?"

"No, I have the gender reveal tonight. Tati just mentioned it, man."

Sam knows I'm avoiding my club and have been for months. "Dude, are you okay? Did something happen?"

I want to say that, "*Yeah, something did happen. A petite woman knocked me on my ass by simply existing in my vicinity.*"

But instead, I just give him a basic answer. "Nothing happened. Just not in the right headspace for the club."

He heads out, and I stretch my legs by walking to the kitchen, where Irina is already preparing for the large group that we'll have for dinner.

"Need any help, Irina?"

"From the man who burns water? Nope. You can sit down and eat some of the leftover salad I made your mother for lunch, though. I ran out of fridge space." She points to where a plastic container sits.

Grabbing a fork, I sit at the island to eat the salad and gossip with the woman who helped my parents raise us. Irina, after her husband passed away, moved in with my brother to help take care of Tati and Alexandra. She's the best, and we'd be nowhere without her.

CHAPTER 2

MARIAH

Trying to close out your inbox before lunch should be considered a herculean task with how quickly it fills back up, but I give it my best shot. I'm the head coordinator for a high-end nanny agency in Chicago. I love my job. Plus, I get to work remote, which is even better. I work well alone; being in my own space makes me feel productive and safe. Checking the bottom right corner of my computer, I realize I'm late to my weekly call with my half brother, Juan.

For the past three months, I've been texting with my paternal half brother. About a month ago, we started calling each other on Fridays during lunchtime. It's been interesting to get to know someone who's related to me. I haven't had that since I was a teenager.

Growing up, it was always just me and my mom, Sylvia. She didn't talk to her parents, and they died when I was in elementary school. I don't have a father listed on my birth certificate. My mother refused to tell me who he was and she'd hold his name over me like a dangled carrot until she finally abandoned me when I was sixteen.

If not for Mason and Sarah Jacobs, I'd have ended up in foster care. Sierra's parents wasted no time petitioning the courts for guardianship after my mom abandoned me, and I lived with them from that moment on. I never had a normal parental relationship until I began living with them.

My mother was a severe alcoholic, and now that I'm an adult and better understand behaviors, I wouldn't be shocked to find out drugs were also involved. We never had money and the bills were barely paid. Past-due notices regularly appeared in our mailbox and we had our utilities shut off regularly. But what I could always count on was my mother bringing home creepy men who would try to touch me, and my mother berating me for supposedly stealing her boyfriends. That started happening more frequently as I hit puberty—slight touches on my hip or lingering stares, none of it welcomed or consented to. My mom would regularly get jealous of their attention being on me and would berate me for it, regardless of whether we were alone or not.

The latter was her reason for skipping town with her latest meal ticket at the time, and basically telling me to figure it out. I remember crying as I read the note she'd left me to find. Her leaving left me distraught, but I also had this weird sense of relief. It's a long story, but when I called Sarah, she came over right away.

Mason, Sierra's dad, was driving when they pulled up. They noticed that my mom's car was missing. It was a beat-up Toyota Corolla that barely ran, but that tipped off both of them, since my mom didn't have a steady job. She hadn't had a regular job for years. I can remember Sarah helping me send the application so I could get free breakfast and lunches at school. I had refused to let them pay for me, so she made sure I was taken care of.

Between my call, my tears, and my mom's car missing, Sarah asked me if I was alone. I nodded, too afraid to say the words out loud. She didn't say anything, but she held me in a tight embrace while Mason called the police. I went to their place that night and went to school as normal the next day. When Sarah picked us up from school, she told me that she and Mason had gone and cleaned out the apartment, taking what was mine, and unpacked it in their spare bedroom. I can remember that conversation in the car like it was yesterday.

Sarah calmly explained some of the heavier logistics. "We called CPS, and we filled out an emergency placement request. Someone is waiting with Mason at the house. We will protect you, Mariah."

"I'm sorry." I couldn't look her in the eye. I was a mixture of embarrassed, relieved, scared, and a whole slew of emotions.

"Look at me, sweetheart." I looked at her in the mirror of the car. "You are family to us, and we'll never let anything happen to you."

She didn't lie. The social worker saw their home and the room they gave me, and after an interview with them, granted Mason and Sarah emergency custody. Months of court hearings followed that day, but Sierra's parents never wavered in their love and support of me. I became a second daughter to them. They tried to undo sixteen years of trauma by providing me with family and stability.

Despite the Jacobses' best efforts, I've been shy around men and never trusting towards new people. Living with them was the first time I trusted a man. Mason helped teach me self-defense and that it's okay to trust people. I've been selective with that, but I know that I can trust the Fedorovs.

When Mason and Sarah died during our junior year of college. Their loss hurt me just as deeply as it hurt Sierra. We mourned their loss together, and still do if I'm being completely honest. I know they would still be here if they could, but at the time it felt like just more people who left me.

Abandonment is a fear that never fully goes away. And to make sure I'm never abandoned again, I'll keep my circle as small as possible.

Since my circle is small and men make me nervous, I'm sitting at my desk as a twenty-eight-year-old virgin. I've never really dated aside from some dates in high school that went badly once they realized I was a freak who wouldn't be able to kiss them.

In college, I didn't even try. I'm okay with being alone. Or at least I was okay with it until I met Nikolai Fedorov. I know he'd never want me, but from a distance I try to sneak a peek at him. His longer hair, which he puts up into a bun when he's stressed, or the glasses he wears, are more than enough to keep my attention.

I can tell Sierra's caught me checking him out, but I don't think she'll ever call me on it in case it spooks me. It scares me too, if I'm being honest. Feeling attracted to someone isn't something I've ever acted on, and Niko is no different. My crush on him will pass eventually, just like all the others have before. I know that I'm meant to be alone so I don't get hurt or hurt them. But if there was someone I'd break that plan for, it'd be Niko.

After a few rings, my half brother, Juan answers the phone. "Hey, Sis, how's your week going?"

"Hi, Juan. It's good. Work's insanely busy this time of year since people need more childcare with all the parties and events for the holidays. How's work for you?"

"It's going well. I'm looking forward to Christmas. My mom always makes the best food." I can practically see the smile on his face when he talks about his mom.

"I love the holidays too, especially when we get a white Christmas. The snow makes it feel so much more cozy."

Getting to know Juan these past few months has been everything I could've dreamed of. He's younger than me by about four years, making him twenty-four. Our father's name is Felipe. He's married to Juan's mother, Camila.

I've also learned that I had a younger half sister—Bianca. She passed away nine years ago and it breaks my heart that I'll never get to meet her. Juan has told me a lot about her. He says that she was the funniest person he's ever met and that she wanted to join the family business too, despite our dad's reservations.

Juan graduated from UCLA with a degree in chemistry, and he works for our dad just like Bianca wanted to. I don't know what business they run, but I figure I'll learn in time. I haven't gotten to meet Juan in person yet. I think that's on both of us to be honest.

I wasn't sure I was going to even reach out, let alone develop a sibling relationship. I want to be cautious, despite how excited I was to know that there was someone genetically tied to me out in the world. And on his end, he hasn't told the family he found me. When I learned that our father was married, I was hesitant. I don't want to disrupt their lives or cause issues in their marriage. Juan's assured me that wouldn't happen, but I haven't wanted to risk it.

He says that his mother already knows there's a possibility I exist. Juan's told me that our father has always said that he dated a woman who ghosted him after only a couple of months of being together. She left him a few weeks after a broken condom. He said Felipe always wondered if she was pregnant. Unfortunately, since it was the early 90's, it was harder to track people down. Given that it was such a short fling, he tried to forget, but hated that never knew for sure if he had an older child.

Knowing that my mom ghosted my dad isn't shocking, and it's likely the truth. She's been flaky since she was a teenager, from what I can tell. She was pregnant with me when she was twenty-two, so the timelines fit and the DNA test doesn't lie.

Changing the subject, Juan shocks me with his suggestion. "I was thinking that maybe we set up a time to meet in person before the holidays."

His idea brings a smile to my face. "That'd be really nice, Juan. I was thinking that it felt like a good time to meet up, too. Maybe for lunch or something?"

"Yeah, that'd be great. I'll want to tell our dad and my mom soon, too."

"Okay, if you're sure that they won't be upset by the news, it'd be really special to meet them as well."

"It'll be fine, Sis. I promise. I'll talk to you next week and we can set up a time, okay?" Every time he calls me, sis, I swear my heart flutters. To be someone's sister is more than I ever hoped for. But I'm glad he wasn't with me when I was a child. I wouldn't wish my childhood on even my worst enemies.

"Works for me. Bye, Juan."

He hangs up and not even a minute later my phone rings again. Thinking it's Juan calling back, I answer right away.

A deep voice that I don't recognize starts to speak. "Watch your back. Not everyone will buy that innocent act of yours. You know what you're doing isn't right, bitch." Heavy breathing continues on their side of the call.

I hang up immediately and block the number from my phone. Shit, that's the seventh creepy call I've gotten in the last couple of months. It's always a different voice and a weird, cryptic message that doesn't make any sense.

Even though I'm creeped out, I still need to finish up my workday. Crossing off a few meetings and to-dos, I wrap up my Friday a few minutes early so I can jump in the shower and get ready for Sierra's gender reveal tonight.

Ever since Sierra moved in with Misha and the girls, I've moved my things over to the larger bedroom. We shared a two-bedroom, two-bathroom condo in the West Loop of Chicago. I love this condo, we'd lived here for a few years, and the location is great.

We didn't have to live together. We both made more than enough to live on our own, but it was nice to not eat dinner alone or watch crappy reality TV shows by myself. I'm so happy that she found Misha, though. He loves her fiercely, and my friend deserves nothing less.

Moving into Sierra's old room allowed me to convert the second bedroom to be my full-time office space. I previously worked in a small alcove in our living room, but now I get to spread out a little bit and enjoy the sunlight from a large window while I work.

After I rinse the workday off, I do some light makeup and find a pair of jeans to go with my favorite deep purple cardigan. I throw on a basic white tee underneath and grab a pair of gym shoes. Finding my purse, I lock up the condo and head downstairs.

I order an Uber over to the Fedorov house, and on the drive over, I sit in the back seat of the car that picked me up and smile. My best friend is going to be a mom. I think she'd already consider herself a mother figure to Misha's daughters, but this baby will be hers. She's twenty-three weeks along, and we're all excited to find out what she's having.

I know Sierra's always wanted to be a mom. She's exactly like Sarah was—kind, loving, and supportive. I decided a long time ago that being a mother wasn't something that I wanted. Besides the fact I didn't have men I trusted in my life, I wasn't going to be anything like my own mother. I would much rather be an aunt who gets to spoil kids and love on them, while keeping a distance when I need to.

I struggled too much growing up, and despite spending years in therapy trying to cope with the deep wounds that are left on my psyche, I know that being a mom is more than I can mentally give. I don't trust myself enough to not end up like my mom. I realize it sounds irrational, but until Niko, it didn't matter.

Speaking of Nikolai, I have a request for my favorite Fedorov brother. I know that he probably thinks of me as Sierra's weird friend, but my request is something I've given a lot of thought to. I'm hoping I can convince him to take my virginity.

What I've learned about Nikolai Fedorov, over the last six months, is that he's trustworthy and wouldn't ever do anything to harm me. I also know that he owns a sex club here in the city, where he only partakes in activities with contract submissives. Sierra let it slip a few weeks ago that Niko is currently between subs, making this the perfect opportunity to finally lose my virginity to someone who will keep it professional.

I realize that sounds contradictory, but I basically want someone I'm familiar with and trust without needing to date them or anything. I know I don't want kids, and that's a deal-breaker for a lot of people. I'd rather lose it with someone I know and am attracted to, hence my proposal to Niko.

I want to lose it by my twenty-ninth birthday in January. He's my best bet, and from what Sierra's told me, Niko has tried to flirt with me before. I don't know that I believe her, but I do know that if Niko won't do it, I'll ask him to set me up with someone else at his club who he thinks could be a good match. But either way, I will be free from this social construct. I can finally have something to compare my self-induced orgasms to. I also would like to have someone teach me in a low-pressure setting, making Niko my best available option.

The Uber driver pulls off to the side of the street by the gatehouse. He looks wary—most people are, but I'm completely safe in my approach. Ilya waves to me as he opens the gate. He's driven me home a few times since he lives a few blocks from my condo. He's a sweet kid, fresh out of high school. Even though he's young, I know the family trust him implicitly.

When I head through the front door, Alexandra greets me with a smile and leads me straight to the kitchen where Irina, their house-keeper, and Anastasia, Niko's mom, are cooking dinner. Both come to kiss my cheek.

"What can I help with?" I say as I throw on an apron.

"Can you chop some of the broccoli and cauliflower? I'm going to give them a good roast in the oven," Irina says, taking me up on my offer.

"Easy enough," I say as I get set up to help prep dinner.

The girls are flitting around with Anastasia as they try to decorate the large dining room. I can tell how hard they're working to make this special for Sierra and their new sibling.

After an hour of helping Irina get dinner ready, in walks Sierra. "Mariah, you're here!" My best friend greets me with a big hug that hits a little differently now, since her baby bump started to show last week.

"I am." I laugh as she adjusts the front of her outfit. I ask her, "How did the appointment go?"

"Went well. Baby is measuring right on target and I feel good. Just woke up from a nap. I just enjoyed a cookie that I intercepted off Vlad, who was sneaking a handful to his office."

This pregnancy has my best friend fiending for sweets. She has always been a salty or savory person, so to see her jonesing for cookies is hilarious.

"It's time! I'm going to get Dad and our uncles. Go to the dining room, everyone," Alexandra directs us.

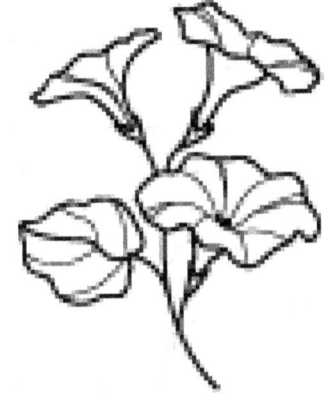

CHAPTER 3

NIKO

Sam left Misha's to head back to our main office in the Loop earlier this afternoon. I've been slowly chipping away at some administrative tasks since then. I pull my glasses from my face, before rubbing my eyes. Staring at a computer all day makes me a little restless. I'll be sure to text my brother Toly after we leave here tonight, and see if he wants to go to the gym with me. I have a lot of pent-up energy from spending the last couple of days trapped in my office ahead of the holidays.

Even though I'm Bratva trained, I've never been one to jump into danger like my brother Misha, or our cousin Vlad. I prefer to stay behind the scenes when I can. But don't take that to mean I won't kill whoever I need to in order to protect my family and our men. I'm Bratva to my core; it's in my blood.

Pulling me from my thoughts, I hear my niece, Alexandra, shouting down the office wing to anyone who's still over here that it's almost time for the gender reveal. I throw my laptop into my leather messenger bag so I can leave after dinner before closing my office door.

I walk into the large family room and sit on the sectional couch next to my cousins, who have a hockey game on the big TV. My dad is behind me, playing a game of chess with Toly. But my eyes are drawn to the room's newest occupant: Mariah.

She greets everyone just as the girls come in behind her to direct us all to head towards the dining room. We all walk in to find decorations everywhere. They were able to get pink and blue streamers on the ceiling, balloons everywhere, and little pieces of confetti on the table.

"Girls, this looks great," I tell my nieces, who are thrilled everyone is so excited about learning the gender of their new sibling.

"They did an amazing job. We only supervised this afternoon; they did all the work. I'm so proud of both my granddaughters." My mom gives them both a proud smile.

My parents were never shy with showing affection to us, and to each other. Despite being a Bratva family, they wanted us to enjoy our childhoods. I have thanked them both over the years because I've seen other kids, in various other crime families, not be so lucky.

I look over to where Mariah is standing. She's playing with the edge of her sweater as she talks to Irina. Fuck, she's so beautiful, and it really pisses me off that she didn't grow up with love around her like we did. I want to show her that being with someone doesn't mean giving up independence. That the right person will ensure she can live her absolute best life.

That last thought is crazy in itself, considering that up until six months ago, I never dreamed of being with a woman outside of the club or outside of a contract. Mariah is the difference, and it's why I have been dragging my feet on finding a new sub.

I can't think of any other woman. Each time I've jerked off the last few months, it's been to thoughts of her. I guess I should take the hint that since she's never reciprocated my flirting, it's probably time to begin the selection process and compile a list of potential subs.

Bringing my focus back to the party, Alexandra is passing around a tray of vanilla frosted cupcakes.

"Okay, everyone, on the count of three we'll all take a bite from our cupcakes. If it's a boy, there'll be blue filling, and for a girl, it'll be pink." Tati instructs everyone on what to expect before Alexandra begins the count.

On three, everyone bites and cheers start erupting. I pull away from my own cupcake and see the bright pink frosting coming out of the middle. I smile because, in just a few short months, I'll have another niece.

I set my cupcake on the table so that I can share my congratulations. I give my brother a big hug, and give Sierra a kiss on the cheek. Misha is an amazing dad already. I know this little girl will have him wrapped around her tiny little fingers.

My nieces ask Misha and Sierra if they have any names picked out. Looking at each other, my brother gives his wife a nod and Sierra responds, "We do have a name. We're going to call her Kira Elena."

Tati and Alexandra start to tear up and run to Sierra and their dad. Paying homage to Misha's first wife, who passed away six years ago, is something that Sierra would do. She's an incredible woman to have embraced the girls' mother like she has.

My parents give them another round of hugs and kisses. My dad, Maxim, is known in many circles as one of the most ruthless men to ever rule a Bratva. Even when he's in Russia, he's a feared man. But in this room, he embraces being a grandpa. I see him wipe a stray tear from his cheek before giving my mom a kiss. Their marriage was arranged as well but, as they tell us, it was nearly love at first sight.

They, along with Misha and Sierra, give me hope that one day I'll have someone to come home to. I'd love it if that person was Mariah. I find myself looking around the dining room for her, only to feel someone reach for my arm. I turn my head to find the brunette beauty standing next to me.

"Hey, Niko, after dinner could we talk somewhere private?" she asks me, a blush quickly beginning to cover her cheeks.

"Yeah, sure. We can head to my office, if you want."

"Sounds good. I'll find you after we eat. Thanks." And she quickly walks away, rejoining the rest of my family.

After sitting down, we all enjoy an amazing meal together. Celebrating Sierra and Kira, we all talk about who she'll look like more and Christmas plans, and the girls tell us about the art show that Alexandra is entered in. Being around my family is something I'll never take for granted.

I had almost graduated with my master's degree when I got the call from Toly that Elena had had an aneurysm and passed away. She came into our family as a stranger but, during their marriage, she became a sister to me. She would send me care packages while I was away at school. She would remember how much I love to do puzzles, getting me a new one for every holiday. She took the time to love each of us, and even though she and Misha weren't a total love match like our parents, they loved each other as friends and partners.

After she passed and we attended her funeral, I finished the last week of school before moving back home to Chicago. I actually moved in here, with my brother, to help take care of Tati and Alexandra. He's our Pakhan, and as his younger brother, I'll do anything I can to support him, even if it means stepping up to help care for my nieces in the wake of their mother's death.

I'm pulled from my thoughts as Misha asks me how Tati is doing so far, since she swapped her apprenticeship to work under me.

"She's doing well. I think that she's got really good ideas on modernizing some of the legitimate business tasks. I'm interested to see what she comes up with."

"She was telling me all about it. She said getting to learn from you and Sam has been fun, so far. Let him know that I appreciate him helping her. I'm sure when he became our CFO, he didn't think he'd be teaching my teenager how to launder money." He laughs.

"Sam's known for a while she'll eventually be taking over. I think that he's afraid he'll scandalize her somehow, but I've promised him that she knows every aspect of our business dealings."

"It's crazy to think that my little girl is going on missions already, but we did at her age too."

I smile at that because it's true. Once we got to high school, our parents started letting us go on missions with Dad. "I'll keep you in the loop, but so far so good on her learning the financial aspects."

He pats my back and pulls me in for a hug. "Love you, Niko."

"Love you too. And congrats again. You're an amazing dad, Misha."

Irina stands up, beginning to grab some of the serving platters that cover the middle of the twenty-person dining room table. I grab some myself to help her. When I set them down on the island in the expansive kitchen, she rubs my upper arm lovingly. "You're such a good uncle. This new baby is a real blessing for the whole family."

"You know we love you, Irina." I pull her in for a hug. She may work for us, technically, but this woman is my mom's best friend. She helped to raise all five of us.

Walking back over to the dining room, I see Mariah motioning for me to join her. Like a moth to a flame, my feet work before my brain can even attempt to keep me where I was standing. She's fidgeting, clearly nervous over whatever she's asked to speak to me about.

Everyone else is focused on their own conversations, so I lean in to quietly ask, "Do you want to go to my office now?"

Mariah nods and I lead her out, putting my hand on her lower back. That cute little blush she had earlier returns, sparking a live wire of hope in my mind that maybe my feelings aren't totally one sided.

We make our way through my brother's house to the office wing, where I place my fingerprint on the door to unlock it. Mariah follows me in and heads straight over to the couch before sitting down. I let the door close and join her on the couch.

"I have a favor to ask you." She is clearly nervous as hell, but I sit and prepare to listen. If only she knew that I'd give her anything she asks for.

Chapter 4

Mariah

Now that I'm sitting next to Niko, in his office, I'm officially freaking out. I know that what I'm about to ask him is going to come as a huge shock, especially since he doesn't see me the way that I see him. Steeling myself for likely rejection, I square my shoulders, and mentally prepare to ask him to take my virginity.

I know my plan is a little far-fetched, but I know that he doesn't currently have an exclusive arrangement at Rapture thanks to Sierra being a certified yapper. So he's likely not having regular sex. That can work in my favor.

He'll be a safe option. I can try to keep my feelings for him on lockdown, in favor of having my first time be with someone who'll put my pleasure first. I've never been all that eager to trust other people, but the Fedorovs have all shown me time and time again that they can be trusted. Knowing that, I can say with confidence he would never push me to do more than I'm comfortable with or try to take anything without consent.

If he did, his mom and Irina would put him in an early grave. His dad and brothers would be quickly behind the women if he did do anything I wasn't okay with. Plus, I know that it'd stay private between us if I asked. As I take a deep breath before I jump into this conversation, he interrupts my thoughts.

"Mariah, what'd you want to talk to me about? Are you okay?"

I decide to jump directly in. "I'm a virgin. I want you to take my virginity."

Niko's jaw opens and his eyes are wide as saucers behind his glasses. I decide to give him some context while his brain tries to catch up to what I'm saying. "I know I've talked to you before about how I've never been interested in dating or anything. But I'll be twenty-nine in January and I want to experience sex. I want to try to experience that level of intimacy, to get rid of this weird internal pressure I feel to just get it over with."

"Having sex for the first time isn't something to just mark off from your weekend to-do list. I'm not sure..." His voice fades back to being shocked at my request.

"Please, Niko. I've really thought about this. This isn't a small ask; I get that, I swear. But I know that you're someone I can trust."

"Mariah, I don't know. I don't think this would be a good idea."

I know that I said I was prepared to hear him say no, but it hurts more than I would've thought. I rub my hand over my sternum, trying to not let the sting of being rejected take hold. I know he probably doesn't find me attractive, and likely isn't interested in deflowering a twenty-eight-year-old virgin. Giving it one last shot, I do my best to explain why I asked him.

"I know it's out of left field for you. I'm clearly less experienced than all of your previous partners. I know that I don't look like them either." I bow my head a bit, trying to hide how sad that makes me feel.

Looking at my fingers sitting in my lap, I continue. "I know that you're between partners. I promise that I'd listen and do my best to make sure that you feel good. It might not be like what you're used to, but I would want you to enjoy yourself."

Looking back up at him, I notice immediately the look in his eyes has changed. He's no longer shocked. He almost has this dark look in his eyes. "I promise you that attraction isn't the problem here. You've said before that you don't want to date anyone or have kids. I'm sorry for my initial reaction—I was shocked. And just to be clear, I have no doubt I would thoroughly enjoy myself."

He stands up from where he was sitting on the couch with me. Suddenly, he's dropping to his knees in front of me. I look back down at my hands to avoid eye contact, but he gently puts his fingers under my chin to lift my head and make my eyes meet his own. "Don't you dare think for even a nanosecond that any of them hold a candle to you. You're the sexiest woman I've ever seen. I never want to hear you put yourself down like that again. Do you understand me, Mariah?"

I nod meekly, but that's not good enough for him.

"I need to hear the words, darling."

"I understand. I'm sorry I asked you about this. I thought you might do it, but it's okay. Do you think that someone else at Rapture would be interested?"

"No. They will not be interested."

"Oh." Feeling really defeated, I nod and try to stand up from the couch, but Niko blocks me from leaving.

He runs his hand through his hair, taking a deep breath. I almost don't want to hear what he'll say next. He looks directly at me as he says, "I'll do it. Only if you sign a contract. All of this will only take place at Rapture."

"A contract?" Whoa, he's actually agreeing! Hell yes.

"Yes. The only way I'll do it is if you agree to a dom/sub contract with me. If you want me to teach you, this is how we'll do it. Take a few days to think about it, okay?"

"If I decide to agree to sign something, then what?"

"Then we'll meet to discuss and negotiate every detail. From everything about what you're comfortable with to what your limits are, and what you want to try. We'll also talk about what you don't want to try."

YES! This is exactly what I was hoping for. I feel a sense of immediate relief flooding my body. "I don't need time to think about it. I'll do it. I'll be your new submissive."

He gives me a simple nod of his head. "Very well. Meet me at noon on Monday, at the Fedorov Industries main office. We'll discuss everything then."

"Can we keep this between us? I don't want to tell Sierra or have her find out. I want this to be just for me."

"I can live with that." He moves out of the way so we can rejoin everyone celebrating baby Kira.

We head back to the dining room and find it empty. We hear voices in the large family room, meaning everyone must've moved somewhere more comfortable. Not the least bit surprisingly when we walk in, we see the rest of the family is playing a game of blackjack. This family really loves their games.

"Deal me in?" Niko asks, causing everyone to look directly at us as we join them. Dima, who's dealing, nods his head and points to where Niko should sit. I stand back, observing this large family. It makes me wish I'd had something like this growing up. There's so much love here. I didn't experience anything like this until I moved in with Sierra in high school.

I can still remember when my mom left. I came home from school one day to find a couple of broken liquor bottles on the ground in the kitchen. That typically meant my mom had run out of alcohol and got mad about it. I quietly cleaned it up in case she was passed out in her room. I learned after a few backhands to the face that waking her up was never worth it. I went straight to my room and locked the door, just doing my homework.

I came back out a few hours later after finishing an essay to realize it was still quiet. I cautiously went to go look for her and I noticed that her room was empty. All of her things were gone, not even a sock left behind. I pulled out the pay-per-minute phone to try calling her. It immediately said, "This number is not in service."

Walking back through the kitchen, I saw the note on the front of the refrigerator.

Jeff doesn't like kids, so I'm moving out. Do not try to find me.

Oh, and don't think I didn't see you trying to get with him this weekend either. You're such a slut. Better keep your legs closed or you'll end up knocked up like I was. I regret having you every single day.

The tears blurred my vision as I called Sierra's mom, Sarah. She came right over and brought Mason with her. It was the first time an adult had shown up for me when I really needed one. They ended up calling the police when they found out I was alone and had been left by my mom. I went home with them, never leaving until college.

After zoning out, I hear my name. I find Tati standing in front of me. "Mariah, did you want to play?"

"Thanks, but I think I'm going to head out." I walk over to Sierra and give her a tight hug. Misha comes over to give me a courteous embrace. I make my rounds to say goodbye to everyone. I grab my purse and coat from the hallway closet. This time of year in Chicago can be brutal, so I'm sure to also put on the hat I tucked into the pocket of my coat.

As I reach for the door, Ilya comes into the foyer. "Heading home, Mariah?"

"Yeah, I was going to order an Uber."

"No worries, I'll drive you."

"You sure?"

"Of course. Let's go." He opens the front door and leads me to his SUV.

Ilya is a nice kid. I know he's a guard for Misha. He's driven me home a couple of times before. His apartment is only a few blocks from my condo over in Fulton Market. Sierra says he's climbing the ranks quickly. I can tell he's a hard worker who has a deep respect for their organization and Mikhail.

We talk during the drive home about the newest addition to the family and our upcoming holiday plans. I'm sure to thank him as I get out of the car and head into my condo.

***

Wanting to take my time getting out of bed this morning, I read the newest book off my TBR list. After an hour, I finally give in to my need for coffee and food. After starting the coffee maker, I grab some ingredients for a quick omelet. I love to cook. After having to take care of meals on my own so often growing up, I got pretty decent at it. My baking skills could use some finesse, but I'm sure I'll make some cookies with Irina as we get closer to the holidays.

Wanting to read while I eat breakfast, I'm on my way to go to my room to grab my book when I hear my phone ringing back at the table. I race back to pick it up thinking that maybe it's Sierra. But it's a random number.

Occasionally I'll get unknown numbers calling me because of my job. I schedule for so many nannies and families that every so often someone will get a hold of my personal number. Not wanting to miss the call, I answer it and immediately regret it.

I hear the same heavy breathing as I did on the call yesterday. The hairs on the back of my neck are ramrod straight. The voice begins to talk. While the voice is different, it sounds just as menacing and threatening.

"Stop talking to him now before you regret it, you stupid whore. I'll make sure you regret it."

"Who is him? Who are you talking about?"

I don't get an answer because the caller hangs up. I put my phone down and try to take some deep breaths because I'm officially freaking out. That's the second call I've gotten in two days. The calls have never been that close together before. Sometimes there's a couple weeks between them.

I wanted this to just go away on its own, but it's clearly not. I let my breakfast and coffee go cold while I continue to sit at the table staring at my phone. I really don't want to tell Sierra. She's pregnant and already has so much on her plate. I'm also not sure what I'd even say because all I've had are some weird phone calls. It could be a prank.

Talking myself through a plan, I promise to talk to Misha if it escalates further. I know he'll help. He'd fix whatever problem I have because he's told me that still owes me for saving Alexandra back in July.

I really didn't do anything that special. I refused to let her run from the spa that day without her shoes. I didn't care about myself in those moments. Sierra had given herself up so that me and Alexandra could try and escape from that crazy woman, Nikita.

I feel better knowing that if there's anything more, I'll go to Misha so he can handle it.

After I clean up the cold food and dirty dishes, I go to take a shower so that I can run some errands. With a list of things I need to get done this weekend, I start by making my way over to my favorite boutique. I want to get something special to wear for Niko. The lingerie in this store is luxurious. I walk in and the sales associate asks if I need any help. I let her know that I'm just browsing.

Moving from table to table, I eventually find a very sexy red bra and panty set. It's cut high on the thigh. I regret not telling Sierra about my plan. She's by far the more sexually experienced between the two of us, and would've been able to tell me if this would be a good choice to wear for Niko.

The sales associate comes up after watching me stare at the same set for the past couple of minutes. "While I think that color would look amazing on you, your figure would be absolutely insane in this bodysuit that we just got in. Hold on right here."

She heads to the back storeroom to find her recommendation and when she comes back out, I know right away that I'm going to buy it. It'll make my B-cup breasts look great. The color is the same red as the set I was looking at.

"The thigh cut on this will look better on you than the set you had. I also think the way this has a belt detail would snatch your waist and make you look phenomenal," she explains.

"I love this. Can I try it on?" With that she leads me to the fitting rooms, and it turns out she selected the perfect size for me. Looking in the mirror, I genuinely like who I see staring back. She looks confident. I quickly put my own clothes back on before meeting her back out in the main section of the store.

"This is exactly what I was looking for. Thanks for your help." I set the bodysuit on the checkout counter for her to ring me up.

After paying, I start to do the rest of my errands, stopping by Trader Joe's and picking up a package at the lockers down the street.

Once I'm back home and have put everything away, I grab the bag from the boutique. I lay the lingerie out on my bed. While I still stand firm on not having kids, I do think that if there was ever someone that

I'd want to be with more than just sexually, it'd be Niko. I just really hope I don't disappoint him.

I don't want him to regret sleeping with me or anything like that. I want to be a good submissive. In the spirit of research, I grab my laptop and begin looking up more about Rapture, BDSM, and having a dom. I want to go into this meeting on Monday prepared and as composed as I can be. I want to impress him, and hopefully make him eager to get me into bed.

CHAPTER 5

NIKO

I start my workday by walking into my office at Misha's house. I sit down in front of my monitors, and I try my best to focus for the next couple of hours. Endless amounts of paperwork, emails, and other bullshit administrative tasks bog me down until Vlad knocks on my door.

"Morning. Do you mind coming to the conference room? Pakhan wants to walk through some stuff that's left over from Kuznetsov transfers."

"Yeah, I'll be right there."

Standing up, I fix my shirt and notice on my watch that it's only ten. I still have two hours to kill before I see Mariah again. When I leave my office, I turn right to meet up with my brothers in the larger conference space.

Our cousins, Vlad and Dima, were raised alongside us after their parents were killed when we were kids. I view them to be as much my brothers as I do Misha and Toly.

When I walk into the conference room, I take my seat next to them all. I open my laptop so that my oldest brother can start this meeting.

"Niko, can you pull up the list of assets we drafted? I want to finalize the last distributions," Misha requests.

Pulling up the file, I grab the remote for the large TV that's hung on the far wall so that I can share my screen. Once I have the document up for them to see, we spend the next hour delving into the remaining pieces left to break up after our family demolished the Kuznetsovs.

My brother married Elena Kuznetsov nearly fifteen years ago. She passed away in her sleep, leaving my two nieces without their mother. Elena and Misha were in an arranged marriage that was secured via an alliance our fathers negotiated. While my brother wasn't in love with Elena, he loved her as the mother of his girls and as a close friend. She was close with all of us. She was my sister. I miss her a lot, but I'm so glad that we've got Sierra now, too.

Over the summer, Sergei Kuznetsov, Elena's dad, tried to kidnap Tati and eventually also tried to kidnap Alexandra. Sierra managed to protect the girls both times—a feat that we're still incredibly impressed by. She's almost as good of a shot as I am. But during all of this, we managed to kill Sergei and his top assassin, Nikita Orlov.

His empire crumbled quickly. He had already lost most of his power after his younger son died unmarried and childless. His soldiers could all see the writing on the wall. It didn't help that the man was losing his fucking marbles. He thought he could take on the Fedorov Bratva and win.

Toly spent a month in New York working with our allies to make sure that a power vacuum didn't develop in the wake of Sergei's death. We also prioritized making sure the Bratva families that benefited from his death were as staunchly against human trafficking as we are. The despicable business was one of the Kuznetsov Bratva's main streams of revenue. My family made it our mission to save as many people as possible. We fucked over Sergei every chance we got, and the families who received other pieces of his business assured us that they will tell us whenever someone comes lurking for new routes to traffic people.

"Okay, I'll call their Pakhan and make sure it gets handled. Toly and Vlad, you guys sure you'll be able to go back to New York at some point in January?"

Vlad responds for them both. "Yeah, we're good. I'll try to do the trip before the girls go back to school from winter break."

Vlad is our chief enforcer and head of security. He personally oversees the girls' safety. He'd rather die than let anything happen to them. He almost did when Sergei kidnapped him and Sierra. They both obviously survived, but Vlad's knee was pretty fucked up. He also had dozens of cuts to his torso that were given to him when Sierra wouldn't give Sergei the information he wanted.

"Great. I think we've finally put all this shit to rest. I'll let you know what they say, but plan for that trip, yeah?"

"Understood." Toly nods at our brother.

My watch vibrates as my alarm goes off. It's time to leave so I can meet with Mariah. I hit the button on the side of my watch to silence it and I close my laptop. We ended the meeting, so I walk back into my office and throw my computer in my messenger bag.

I let Misha know that I have some meetings over at the main offices in the Loop, but I'll be back here tomorrow.

"Sounds good, man. Love you, Niko."

"Love you too, Bro."

Quickly walking outside to my car, I wave to Ilya at the gatehouse as I turn onto the street. Making the drive over to the Fedorov Industries' building, I turn the car to head down to the underground parking deck. I'm starting to hum with excitement as I make my way up to the executive floor. I smile at everyone I see, because in less than ten minutes I'll be seeing Mariah.

I spent all day yesterday thinking about Mariah and what I agreed to do. Her asking me to take her virginity was a shock, to say the least. I sort of figured she'd be inexperienced, but I never in a million years would've thought she would ask me to be her first time. It's no secret in the family that I own Rapture and I'm sure Sierra's told her about my arrangements.

But they don't know the reason I haven't slept with anyone for over six months. Nobody knows the feelings I've harbored for Mariah since the minute I set eyes on her that day we went to the Art Institute. I figured this whole time that she was being nice when she'd flirt back occasionally, but to know that she's likely got similar feelings to my own lit a fire of hope inside me.

I initially tried to say no, because I remembered her saying that she was not interested in dating. I didn't want to get attached or let my feelings grow deeper if she couldn't reciprocate fully. But the look on her face when I said no told me that my rejection deeply stung. And when she tried to say she understood that she doesn't look like the women I've been with before, or insinuated that I wouldn't be satisfied or turned on, it had me quickly agreeing to take her virginity.

It hurt me to see her talk so poorly about herself. I decided then that in order to keep my heart out of this, I'll have her sign a contract to be my submissive. That means three months teaching her everything about sex. I get to show her pleasure she's never experienced and help her to take charge of her sexuality within her role as my submissive.

Would I love to have her say she'd be interested in a date with me instead of going to Rapture? Fuck yeah I would, but the secret masochist in me agreed to a club-only arrangement because I cannot fathom not getting to be with Mariah. This contract will help me maintain boundaries to keep my heart safe.

I know Mariah would never hurt me on purpose, but she doesn't know that she holds my heart in her hands.

Walking down the hallway towards Sam's office, I pass by his assistant, Erin. I give her a wave. She's worked for us the past twelve years or so, well before Sam or I started here. She's incredible at her job and Sam would be lost without her. His inability to be on time is only fixed because Erin will drag him wherever he needs to be.

I close Sam's door behind me as I set my bag down next to his desk.

"Morning to you too, bro," he snarks.

"I need to use your printer," I say gruffly. Opening my bag and pulling out the laptop, I quickly navigate to the document that my lawyers crafted when I decided to partake in Rapture myself after it opened. I wanted to make sure that my subs were completely protected and understood my boundaries. It's a lengthy contract, but it allows both parties to be confident in our dynamics and have a complete awareness of what is consented to and what isn't.

I begin to print out the document, and as it finishes, Sam asks me what I'm printing.

"A new contract. Mariah will be here soon. I'll need complete privacy in my office. Can you have Erin guard the door to make sure I'm not interrupted?"

"Mariah? As in Mariah Perez? Sierra's best friend?" Sam's stunned at my admission.

"Yes," I say simply. I promised her that I'd keep it private. Sam will never say anything to anyone about this arrangement. He understands what's at stake. Plus, if anyone could guess my feelings for her, it'd be Sam.

"Is that smart?"

"Probably not, but she asked me to do her a favor and when I initially said no, she then asked if someone else at Rapture would be interested. Over my dead body would I let some other fucker touch her. So, I agreed."

"Interesting. You want her more than just as a sub, don't you?"

Fucking called it. This man misses nothing. I guess it doesn't help we've been friends our entire lives.

"I do, but it's complicated, man. She's jumpy and untrusting of almost everyone. I just want her to be safe, even if I can't have her the way I'd really like to."

"Just be careful, okay? I'd hate to have to drink you through heartbreak," he jokes. I throw a pen at him.

A knock on his office door reveals Erin. "Hey, Nikolai, there's a Mariah Perez waiting for you? I set her up in your office, if that's alright?" At a normal office, I'm sure it wouldn't be good etiquette to put a visitor in an office unsupervised, but Erin knows that my office is largely empty. I don't even have a filing cabinet in that room.

"That's perfect. Thanks, Erin." Grabbing the contract off the printer, I follow her back out to the main area of our executive floor. I see that the door to my office is open. I knock to announce myself, and as Mariah turns around, the wind gets knocked out of me.

She's so fucking beautiful. Her warm brown eyes are like a siren's song, holding my attention whenever she's near me.

"Good morning, Mariah. How are you?"

She smiles back at me. "Good. I'm a bit nervous if I'm being honest, but also excited."

"There's nothing to be scared of. This is just to outline everything we're okay with, what is off limits, and other things like frequency and protection."

She nods, but doesn't hide the same fidgeting her fingers did on Friday when she asked me to start this whole thing.

"I've used this same contract for years. It's comprehensive, but worth it when we get on the other side of it. I take my role as a dominant very seriously. Your comfort and safety are my top priorities. Well, along with your pleasure."

That last bit has another blush crawling up her neck. It's the first time I notice her outfit. She's wearing a deep purple sweater dress and tights. I know it's not overly sexy, but it has my cock getting hard regardless. I know it's not because of her clothes. It's her. It's Mariah.

"Do you feel comfortable and ready to get started? Any questions before we start?"

"No. I'm sure I will have questions during the walk-through, but nothing right now."

I nod and slide her copy of the contract over to her while I sit behind the desk. We begin going over the contract, line by line.

Dominant & Submissive Agreement

This contract, between Nikolai Fedorov (dominant) and Mariah Perez (submissive) represents an exclusive, consensual, sexual, power exchange relationship between the aforementioned parties.

1. This relationship is entered into with an understanding that both parties are consenting adults who are of sound mind, agreeing of their own free will. This contract serves as a written outline of the expectations, boundaries, and commitments between the dominant and submissive. This is not meant to be legally binding or enforceable. Either party retains the right to end this agreement at any time for any reason. The relationship between dominant and submissive must put trust and mutual respect at the forefront. Both parties should exercise transparent communication and acknowledge that submission is a gift that must be given, not a right to be taken by the dominant.

2. **Term**

   a. Agreement to a three-month relationship, ensuring

---

the goal submissive has for a birthday wish is met and exceeded.

3. Fundamentals

a. Consent

    i. All meetings, interactions, and communications must be consensual. Consent may be revoked at any time without blame, judgment, or repercussions.

b. **Confidentiality**

    i. Both parties agree to maintain absolute privacy. No details shall be shared with a third party without prior consent by the other participant. If submissive wishes to share with Sierra Jacobs, she has freedom to do so.

c. **Exclusivity**

    i. For the duration of the entire term, both parties shall agree to not enter into any other dynamics or relationships.

d. **Location Boundaries**

    i. All meetings shall take place within Rapture. Texts and phone calls wherever applicable may be allowed to arrange and adjust meetings when necessary.

e. **Frequency**

   i. Dominant agrees to meet up to three times per week for the duration of the contract. Tentative schedule will be Tuesday evenings, Thursday evenings, and Saturday evenings. If adjustments need to be made, either party should communicate and do their best to accommodate any rescheduling.

f. **Safewords**

   i. Both parties should exercise use of safewords when interacting in a sexual manner.

      1. If **Green** is used, both parties are okay and prepared to continue.

      2. If **Yellow** is used, dominant will check in with submissive and correct course based on needs of submissive.

      3. If **Red** is used, dominant will cease activity and end the scene. All applicable toys and implements will be undone to free submissive as quickly as possible.

   ii. **Check-ins**

      1. The dominant will communicate with submissive for regular check-ins through-

out scenes and post-scene to ensure safety and happiness of submissive. The submissive is required to respond honestly to all check-ins.

iii. **Aftercare**

1. Dominant shall provide well-rounded aftercare with submissive. The dominant will arrange for physical and emotional support as needed.

4. **Domains of Control**

a. The dominant's authority extends to the following:

i. Physical positioning and movement of submissive during scenes.

ii. Sexual activities outlined and agreed to prior to scene.

iii. Speech and behavior during scenes.

iv. Rewards and praise.

v. Punishment and corrections.

b. The dominant shall NOT have authority over:

i. The submissive's personal life, where it pertains

to professional life, friends, and family.

ii. Financial matters.

iii. Physical appearance outside of previously mentioned scenes.

iv. Public behavior and statements outside the confines of Rapture.

5. **Acceptable Activities**

a. The following activities are acceptable to both dominant and submissive:

i. Bondage with:

1. Rope, leather, restraints, cuffs, collar.

ii. Sensory deprivation with:

1. Blindfolds and noise canceling headphones.

iii. Sensation play.

1. Feathers, Wartenberg wheel, nipple and clit clamps, vibrators.

iv. Penetration of submissive with:

1. Dildos, plugs, fingers, tongue, penis.

a. Including double penetration and double vaginal penetration.

v. Orgasm control.

vi. Impact play with:

1. Crop, hand, paddle, flogger, belt.

vii. Light discipline .

viii. Role-play: specific scenes will be discussed in advance.

ix. Oral play.

x. Anal play.

6. **Hard Limits**

a. Extreme pain or impact.

b. Permanent marks or scarring.

c. Public exposure.

d. Photography or recording of any kind. However, this can become an acceptable activity if both parties agree to specific scenes prior to activity.

e. Intercourse without protection.

7. **Health**

a. Both parties agree to disclose any medical conditions that may affect the agreement.

b. The dominant will always wear condoms.

c. The dominant shall provide proof of a negative STD screening prior to first scene.

d. The submissive will agree to maintain adequate rest to support safe play.

8. **Termination**

a. Either party is within their rights to terminate this agreement without judgment or penalty.

b. If agreement is terminated early, all records of relationship shall be destroyed.

c. The confidentiality and privacy of both parties will remain in effect in perpetuity.

9. Signatures:

We, the signers, both enter into this agreement freely and with full understanding of its contents. We acknowledge that this document represents the shared interests and boundaries we have as dominant and submissive. We will honor this agreement until the end of the three-month term or until early termination is struck. We also agree that this document is ever changing and items can be added to approved list of activities and items can be put into the hard limits category without judgment or pressure.

Before I hand her a pen to sign the agreement with, I want to make sure that I give her room to ask questions. She nodded along as I read the document out loud. She didn't bat an eyelash at any of the approved activities, so I want to make sure she understood everything.

"Everything look good to you?"

"Yes, I trust you to act in good faith. I don't necessarily have experience with all of the things listed, but I did research over the weekend. I feel confident that, at the very least, I'd want to try everything. I might move some to the hard limits after trying, but it's clear you'll make my comfort a priority, so I'm not worried."

"Of course. Even though you'll be my submissive, you have all the control. The second you say yellow, I'll check in. And if you say red, everything stops. Any parts you want clarification on?"

"No, it all seems pretty straight forward. I appreciate you including the piece about letting me tell Sierra if I want to."

"Full disclosure, my friend Sam Aslanov knows about our arrangement, but him finding out would be inevitable as he's also a member at Rapture. I can assure you that he'll be respectful of your privacy."

She nods. "No worries. I'm guessing he does something similar at the club?"

"Yes. He understands the importance of maintaining boundaries. If you're ready, we can sign both copies now."

She reaches for the cup of pens and happily signs her copy and I spin my copy to face her. When she's done, she passes the pen and contracts to me, where I sign my name next to hers.

I pull out my phone to show her my STD test results. I got tested two months ago, just to be safe, after my previous arrangement at the beginning of summer. I flip it around for Mariah to see the screen.

"These are my last test results; I haven't been with anyone since these were done."

"Okay, thank you. I appreciate it."

"Do you want to set up our first meeting? Tomorrow is Tuesday, just like outlined in the agreement. Does that work for you?"

Her eyes go wide. I think it sets in that she'll be losing her virginity as soon as tomorrow.

"Wow, yeah, no, that works for me. What time should I be at Rapture?"

"Let's do seven. Is that enough time for you after work?"

"That's plenty of time. I'll see you tomorrow. Thank you again, Niko. I appreciate this more than you could ever understand."

No, thank you, sweetheart.

"We'll have fun tomorrow. Can I walk you out?" I stand up from behind the desk to open the door for her. Walking to the lobby area of the floor, Erin stands to go press the button on the elevator. I nod my thanks to her.

"Thanks again, Niko," Mariah whispers as she leans in for a hug. Fuck, she feels so good in my arms. It's like she was meant to be there. The elevator dings its arrival, and she gets onto the car and hits the ground floor button. I give her a wave as the doors close.

I stand there looking at the closed doors, reminding myself that this is a good idea. This will only be at Rapture and the contract is only three months. I can keep my feelings out of it because I don't have a choice.

Mariah says that she's a loner, but I have seen her come out of her shell since she's gotten more comfortable the past few months around my family. I can see how gorgeous she is, how alluring she can be. She has the power to ruin me and she has no clue. I'd never bring this up to her, because I know she had a rough hand dealt to her as a kid, but if she needs me, I'll be there for her no matter what.

***

Walking into my penthouse, I see a note on the kitchen island from my dog walker letting me know that they fed Rasputin around four. Before I can set the note down, the beast comes barreling into my legs.

"Hey, boy. You want to go to the park for a little bit?" He barks excitedly, recognizing the word park. I don't bother to take off my coat. I grab his leash with the small fanny pack that has treats and poop bags. I lead him out of our building and we walk over to the dog park that's a part of a larger green space behind my building. It's a nice fenced-off area where Rasputin loves to run around the play equipment they have in there.

I let him go wild around for half an hour before we head back home. I open my fridge, grateful to see the chef delivered my weekly meals. Popping one into the oven, I text my brother Toly.

> Hey, want to go to the gym in twenty?

> Toly: Yeah, I was just about to head down there, but I'll wait for you.

I give his message a thumbs-up and eat my dinner before changing into some workout clothes. When I open my front door, Toly is waiting outside his door and together we head down to the large gym in our building.

I try to avoid eye contact because my brother is a perceptive motherfucker. I'm distracted after my meeting with Mariah and about what'll happen tomorrow night. He catches on and asks me if I'm okay.

"Yeah, I'm fine. Promise."

"Okay. If you want to talk, you know you can always come to me."

And I do. I know Toly would be there for me in a heartbeat. But he's never really been emotionally comforting, especially after he was kidnapped as a teenager. Going deeper than surface-level feelings has never been his forte. I know he tries, and more importantly, I know he loves me. In this moment, however, I'm glad he doesn't push the topic further.

"I'll see you tomorrow."

"Bright and early." I head back home and leave him to his long treadmill run.

After a quick shower, I climb into bed with Rasputin at my feet. Staring at the ceiling, I fall asleep to scenes of Mariah splayed out, ready and waiting for me. Thank God my dreams will become reality in less than twenty-four hours.

Chapter 6

Mariah

I'm jolted from a deep sleep by the loud alarm currently going off near my head. I scramble to find my phone to make the noise stop. I groan, remembering I set the alarm for thirty minutes earlier than I normally get up so I can do a long everything shower before work.

I wanted to make sure I was as prepared as I could be for whatever tonight has in store. When Niko and I were reviewing the contract, I was squeezing my thighs together. I got incredibly turned on as he read, line by line, all of the things he would possibly want to do with me. It solidified my decision even more. Nikolai Fedorov is the one who'll take my virginity.

I walk into my bathroom, then I start the shower to warm up the water while I grab my exfoliator and razor. Once the water is finally warm enough, I get in and spend the extra time wisely by shaving everything. It's almost giving me a sense of power, like a coat of armor, boosting my confidence. I climb out of the shower and start to dry my hair.

My waves need some extra love with the diffuser attachment on my hair dryer, but I'm more than happy with the end result. I, unfortunately, now have to make it through an entire day of work before I can put on the new lingerie and make my way over to Rapture. I was shocked when he showed me the test results right away because they were dated from a few months ago, meaning he hasn't been with anyone for longer than I thought. I wonder why.

Not going to lie though, I'm nervous. I know that he's an experienced dom and I've barely kissed anyone. I'm harboring a crush that has the ability to break my heart without him ever knowing. I hope these next three months don't hurt me more than help me.

After getting dressed for the workday, I head to my home office and get set up. Opening the blinds, I see that it's a sunny day, but that means nothing in Chicago when it's early December. I know it's likely only thirty degrees out, maximum.

I spend the day bouncing between calls with my team and clients. It can definitely get stressful, but I love the organization of it all. I know that it's a nanny agency, but whenever I solve the day's problems, it gives me a sense of pride in my work for making this place run like a well-oiled machine.

The second the clock on my computer hits five, I'm closing out of everything. I go to make dinner, ensuring that I'm meeting my end of the bargain and showing up to these meetings healthy and rested. Reheating some of the steak I made last night, I watch the latest episode of *Survivor.*

Once I've waited as long as possible before getting ready, I go to my vanity and start to do some light makeup. I know Niko doesn't see me with makeup often, so I figure doing some simple eye liner, mascara, and a muted pink lipstick will be a nice surprise. Feeling content with my final look, I feel like I should do something with my hair. Deciding against it after seeing how good my waves held up throughout the day, I fix my part and fluff my hair. I excitedly turn to the bodysuit that's hanging in my closet.

I put the provocative red lingerie on. It feels luxurious against my moisturized skin. I really hope Niko likes it. Needing to find something to go over the lingerie, I spot a black wrap dress hanging near the back of my closet. I figure that easy access might be simpler, so I pull it off the hanger and adjust my breasts in the dress so everything sits perfectly.

I give myself a once-over in my floor-length mirror. Feeling sexy and confident for the first time in my life, I spray a bit of perfume on the way out. Carefully putting on the knee-high boots I planned to wear, I try to ignore the voice in my head that's telling me I'm not worth his trouble or that he's going to think I'm too much work because I'm nervous.

Relying on the contract to tell my inner hater to go fuck itself, I put on my winter coat, grab my purse, and order my Uber. If there's no traffic, I should get there five minutes early, which is fine. Being late makes my back sweat. My mom never was on time to anything growing up, causing me to be late to school often. If we could be late to something, we usually were. As an adult, I refuse to be late.

Just as I walk outside, my Uber pulls up. Quickly checking that the license plate matches the app, I open the door and greet my driver.

She says she loves my boots, which gives me an extra boost of energy heading into what will likely be an unforgettable night. The drive is short, and we soon pull up to Rapture in River North.

Thanking my driver, I get out of the car and approach the nondescript but still intimidating building. The only marking that indicates its existence is a small plaque near the door. I greet the two security guards standing near the door.

"Evening, ma'am. Can I have your name?"

"Mariah Perez. I'm meeting with Nikolai Fedorov."

He peruses his clipboard of guests they're expecting tonight.

"Yes, Miss Perez, I see you here. Please proceed up the stairs to the lobby and Iris will help you from there." He moves out of the way and opens the door, holding it open for me to walk through.

I climb the staircase, I walk into the opulent lobby area. Everything is sensual and elegant. Beautiful red on the walls, cozy couches, and an inviting counter, with whom I assume is Iris, waiting to greet visitors.

"Welcome to Rapture, Miss Perez. I see it's your first—" But she's interrupted by Niko walking into the room. He's dressed in an all-black suit and shirt combination. He looks hot with his hair pulled back into a bun. I love when he wears it that way, but he looks downright sexy when his hair is down.

"Mariah, it's good to see you. Ready to come on back?" He smiles and motions for me to follow him.

I give him a smile in return, hoping it doesn't let my nerves show through.

I move past his body to enter the main part of Rapture. I stop suddenly, causing Niko to stop at my back. He whispers, "Welcome to the playroom."

60

My mind goes into sensory overload. Everywhere I look, there's something happening. It's a lot to take in, and my eyes ping around the large space. There are men and women having sex on nearly every surface of the room. Moans of pleasure are heard, and I'm unable to distinguish who is letting their pleasure be known.

I see a woman bent over some sort of bench, getting spanked with a flogger. There's a man who's wearing a collar and leash, happily being led around the room by a leather-clad woman.

My eyes dart directly at the floor when I see Niko looking my way. I'm not necessarily ashamed he caught me being a voyeur, but my lingering gaze has me feeling a little embarrassed. He leans closer so I can hear him. "There's nothing to be uncomfortable about in this room. Are you doing okay?"

"I'm good. Just overwhelmed, I guess."

"That's perfectly okay. I have a room saved for us that's private." His hand finds my lower back, and he leads me to our reserved room.

Feeling relieved, I take a deep breath, willing my heart rate to steady. Walking down a long hallway, there are red and green lights above the doors. We stop in front of a door with a green light above it. When we walk in, there's a huge four-poster bed, a dresser that has condoms in a large bowl sitting on top, a couple of chaise longues, and a very big mirror, positioned to face the bed.

"Checking in, Mariah. What color are we at? Remember what the three colors are?"

I quickly remember the stoplight system outlined in the agreement. "Green. I'm green."

"Good girl. I'm going to keep checking in often, okay?"

I nod my response.

He slowly removes his jacket, setting it down on one of the lounge chairs. He walks to the dresser and picks up a couple of condoms, throwing them on the bed. He approaches me, reaching for my coat. He places it on top of his suit jacket.

"Holy fuck, Mariah. You look incredible tonight." It's the first time he's seen my dress. I know the wrap detailing shows off more cleavage than I usually show when I'm with the Fedorovs. Niko reaches for the string that keeps my dress tied. Pulling at it, he carefully strips me of my dress. I free my arms and let it fall to the floor. I'm standing in front of a man for the first time, only in my lingerie and knee-high boots.

"I'm gonna need you to be a good girl for me tonight. I am going to take my time with you. Taking this sexy as hell red bodysuit off of you will be the highlight of my life."

He's saying things that have me wishing our arrangement wasn't tied to a signed contract, but I know that this is the safest for us both.

"I-I wanted to look good for you tonight."

"Mission fucking accomplished, baby."

He reaches to unlatch the bra section of the bodysuit before kneeling in front of me, taking the lingerie with him. He also takes my boots off. I'm officially naked, but Niko is still fully dressed. The power dynamics are making themselves clear already.

"Get on the bed." The look on his eyes has gone dark. The fun-loving and quiet man I've known for the past six months has been replaced by my dom.

I follow his command and get onto the bed facing him as he starts to remove his belt. While he's unbuttoning his shirt, he issues his next order. "I want to see you touch yourself. Put your fingers on your clit and slowly stroke over it."

Watching him get undressed is enough to have my pussy aching for friction. My fingers find their way to my clit as he instructed. He loses his pants and socks before finally coming to join me on the bed. He's still wearing his boxer briefs, but I can finally get a good look at his extensive tattoo collection. He's got intricate patterns covering his entire torso. I can make out the names of his brothers on his right pec muscle.

Lying against me, he puts his hand over where my fingers are still playing with my pussy. I skip a breath at the additional pressure.

"Has anyone touched you here before?"

I shake my head. "No, nobody's ever touched me anywhere. My first and last kiss was in high school."

"You're such a good girl, waiting for me all this time. Saving this for me."

His filthy words have goose bumps developing and covering my entire body. The feeling of his hand taking over for my own has me inching closer to an orgasm. His lips find mine and with a swipe of his tongue, I open my mouth to let him in.

His fingers are magical. I've never felt this good before; neither my bullet vibrator nor my fingers have had me ever feeling this way. I feel like I might explode. Our lips are still connected as he continues to use his hands against my pussy. I can feel him inch towards my opening.

Just as I'm about to cum, he pulls away his hand. "I didn't say you could cum. I also want a taste of this virgin pussy before I destroy it."

He climbs down the bed, crawls between my legs, and asks me, "Color?"

"Still green."

As soon as my answer is out of my mouth, he latches on to my clit and begins to suck. My hips instantly leave the mattress. I've never ever in my twenty-eight years felt the intense heat that starts to form in my core as he continues to feast on me. The feelings he's pulling out of me are almost indescribable.

A noise leaves my mouth before I can stifle it. Niko tilts his head to look at me, but I can still feel his heavy breathing against my pussy. "Don't you dare try to hide your moans from me. I want to hear what I do to you. I want everyone to know who you belong to."

I hear myself begging him "Please, can I cum? Please, Niko, I don't think I can stop it."

"Yes, cum. Cover my face in it." Another thirty seconds of feeling his mouth on my clit has me detonating. It's almost an out-of-body experience. Holy shit, I just had my first orgasm at someone else's hands. Not just an orgasm by anybody; it was by Nikolai's mouth.

I feel his lips kiss my inner thighs before he's getting off the bed. His briefs have a wet spot from where his cock leaked precum. He's turned on by eating my pussy? That's incredibly hot. He yanks his underwear off, grabbing one of the condoms he brought over before we started.

"Are you sure about this, Mariah? I want you to be absolutely positive."

"I promise, I want this. I need you, Niko."

He rips the wrapper off the condom, and rolls it down his cock. As he does, I get my first glimpse at a man's cock in real life. Watching him, I notice just how beautiful he is. He's fully naked, stroking his dick as he walks back over to where I'm lying on the bed, spread open, waiting for him.

CHAPTER 7

NIKO

I reach my hand between us to help guide my cock into the woman I've been fantasizing about for the last six months, inching the head inside her pussy. My cock slowly moves deeper inside of Mariah. I feel the moment I break through what remained of her virginity. She's mine now, whether or not she knows it.

Looking down at her, I ask, "Are you okay?"

"I feel full, and there was a pinch, but now it feels okay. Can I have a second to adjust?"

"Absolutely. You tell me when I can move, yeah?"

She nods and my mind focuses back on how incredible she feels. I can feel her muscles clamping down around me, and it's euphoric. I've been thinking nonstop about this since she asked me on Friday. To have her beneath me now, I could die tonight without a single regret.

"I-I think I'm good now. You can move, Niko."

So I do. I start to slowly build up my thrusting speed. Her eyes close as she lets herself feel everything.

This is the most emotional connection I've ever experienced with a partner. It's all-consuming. I could cum right now from how good she feels. I start doing math problems to make sure I follow through on providing Mariah with a good first time. Leaning my head down to her tits, I suck her nipple into my mouth and run my teeth over it before giving it a little bite between my teeth.

Slightly adjusting my hips so I'm able to thrust fully inside of her, I put my hands on her legs and push them open further. I look down, watching as my cock enters her body during each thrust. I lick my thumb before bringing it to her clit. Starting to rub over the hardened bundle of nerves, I can feel her get tighter and wetter. I let out a moan as she starts to have her second orgasm. "Cum for me, Mariah. Let me feel how much you love my dick stretching out your virgin pussy."

She pulls on the sheets and throws her head back. Just as she rides out her orgasm, my own takes hold. I fill the condom with cum, wishing I could've been inside her bare.

Whoa, where the fuck did that idea come from? I've never once been inside a sub without protection. Deep down, I know it's because Mariah isn't just another sub. For just one shot at being hers, I'd give up nearly everything.

This feeling of intense desire, knowing that I'm her first for every-thing, it's too much. I can feel the panic take hold. I need to get out of here. I'm wishing for things I can't have. I want more than she'll let me have, more than I've ever given to a woman. I need to protect what's left of my heart. I slowly pull out of her, noticing the wince on her face as she feels the loss of my cock. I can't deal with the emotions that have unexpectedly popped into my head, so instead, I try to focus on being her dom.

"Stay here."

Walking to the large attached bathroom, I pull off the condom that's coated in her blood and filled with my cum. Wishing the blood was staining my cock, not the condom, I shake the thoughts from my mind once again. I run a washcloth under the warm water. I bring it back out to her, and I wipe away the blood between her thighs.

Seeing evidence that I will forever keep something of hers is the last straw. I can't do this.

"You can get up and use the bathroom before you leave."

As soon as she closes the door to the bathroom, I rush to get my clothes back on. I haul ass to my office on the main floor to open the liquor cabinet I keep in here. Not bothering with a glass, I drink directly from the whiskey bottle itself.

Furious with Mariah, furious at myself. I keep drinking. I'm in too deep, way over my head. How did I ever think that I could keep my feelings out of this? I hate myself for allowing this to happen. I don't regret being with her, but I regret the contract. I regret the need for me to be the one to take her virginity. Most of all, I regret my response to having my most life-altering, earth-shattering sexual experience with the one woman I can't have.

Having drunk at least a few sips from this bottle to get control of my thoughts, I turn on the security camera footage from the hallway and I see her leaving. Mariah comes into view of the camera, and I can see that her face is red and splotchy.

Fuck. Me. I know I've beyond fucked up this whole night. Aftercare is critical and I just dismissed her. I didn't provide for my submissive, especially after making her sign the agreement. I see the mirror above the liquor cabinet across from my desk. I throw the bottle at the mirror, disgusted by the reflection I see.

She gave me something important. She fucking trusted me. And what did I do? I ran away because I was feeling too much, was feeling too vulnerable. I spat on her trust.

I run out of my office to chase after her. I find her walking through the lobby. "Mariah, please wait!"

She blows right past me, hauling ass down the stairs. Following her, I see Mariah whip the door open and hop into a waiting car. My own car is parked right out front, so I jump inside and follow the car. It doesn't take long to realize she's going straight home. I might've fucked up the entire night, but I will make sure she gets home okay. I'll worry about apologizing tomorrow.

I watch her get out of the car and she walks inside, towards the elevator. I remember her and Sierra saying how slow it is, so I decide to sneak in the back entrance and run up the stairs to the third floor. Waiting in the stairwell, I have a good line of sight to her apartment door without needing to reveal myself. Another minute passes by before she steps up to her front door. She pulls at something taped to the door.

She reads the note, and whatever it says, has her flicking her head down the hallway, almost like she's checking to see if someone is watching her. She fumbles with her keys before unlocking the dead-bolt and her main lock. She gets inside as fast as she can.

I pull out my phone.

> Mariah, I am so sorry. I know I fucked up.

> Please let me make it up to you. I know I failed you. You deserved so much more than me being a cold, distant asshole. I wasn't a good dom tonight when you trusted me and gave me something so precious. I'm deeply sorry. I wish I could tell you what was going on inside my head, but that won't fix my fuckup. I promise you that I will fix this.

Both messages are read, but go unanswered. That's okay—I will earn back her trust, even if I have to break down every wall she tries to rebuild. I know I acted like a complete piece of shit, and it's not okay. She deserves so much better. I'll be better.

I spend all day Wednesday stewing in my self-induced hate. I also manage to order Mariah a large bouquet of wildflowers with a note to be delivered to her condo later this afternoon.

> *Mariah,*
>
> *I'm so sorry about last night. If you give me one more chance, I'd like to explain and make it up to you.*
>
> *I regret my actions and how I treated you. I'll be at Rapture tomorrow night for our scheduled time. I hope you'll show up.*

Yours,

Niko

It takes a lot for me to make through work all day on Thursday, doing as much as I can while thoughts of Mariah consume me. I attempt to avoid Sierra all day, because I'm not sure if Mariah told her about our arrangement, but also because I'm not sure my guilty conscience wouldn't have me blurting out everything that happened.

I'll be heading over to the club later today, hoping she'll show, because I really wanted to focus on oral tonight. I was going to show her how to suck my cock. I wanted to show her more pleasure with my mouth on her body and have her sit on my face. My dick gets hard in my suit pants just thinking about Mariah's wet pussy sitting on my face, suffocating me with her scent.

I didn't text her all day yesterday, giving her some space. I didn't want to overwhelm her more. I only had the florist deliver the flowers. But I want to give her a reminder about tonight, hoping maybe she'll text me back. I'd even accept her anger and hatred. I just can't take not hearing from her. It's agonizing and entirely my fault.

> Mariah, again, I'm so fucking sorry. This was all my fault, and I'd like the chance to make it up to you. I'll be waiting for you at Rapture.

She reads the text, and the typing bubbles pop up but quickly die, leaving me on read once again.

I depart from my brother's house, successfully avoiding not just my sister-in-law, but all of my family. I wave to Ilya as I make my way out of the gate, then I make the quick drive to Rapture. Wanting to get there early, I park and go wait in the bar near the playroom, just off the lobby. As it nears seven, I walk out to the lobby and sit in one of the lounge chairs.

I wait for twenty minutes and start to worry she really isn't going to make it. She's late, but in walks Mariah wearing another one of those fucking wrap dresses that will haunt me until my death. Maybe even into the afterlife. This one is a navy-blue color, still showing ample cleavage. I clench my jaw because I'm reminded just how monumentally I blew it on Tuesday.

I want her more and more every day. But the last two days have me locking down those thoughts in favor of trying to earn back her trust, even if it's just as a friend. I cannot lose her. I know she's not interested in having a family or getting married, but I could live without having kids of my own. Especially if my wife was Mariah.

"Thank you for coming." I hope that my appreciation for her showing up tonight is conveyed.

"I wanted to hear you out. Just know, I don't normally give people second chances."

I hang my head in shame. "I know, and I'm grateful as hell for even a sliver of a chance to make what happened on Tuesday up to you."

I hold out my hand to lead her directly to the room I reserved. I hold the door open to let her enter before me, then I guide her over to the large couch. This room has a similar vibe to the one on Tuesday, but I didn't want one with a bed in case she wasn't interested in that tonight, which would be completely understandable. I wanted her to feel safe and not have a reminder of my failure.

I take a long, deep breath before I give the best effort of my life to apologize for my behavior.

"Mariah, I am so fucking sorry. I truly cannot tell you how much I regret my behavior after what we shared together. What should've been me taking care of you, checking in with you, was ruined because I let my own emotions take over. I've never experienced that as a dom once in my eight years in this lifestyle, and it scared the living shit out of me. I wanted to keep you.

"I know that's not an excuse, just an explanation. How I treated you doesn't deserve a defense. But I felt flayed open by you. For the first time in my life, I wish I could go back in time and not let you walk into that bathroom alone. I really need you to know how deeply sorry I am for how I behaved. You gave me something so fucking special and I hate myself for tarnishing that.

"I know you trusted me and I broke that. I would like to continue our arrangement and I promise to never behave like that or treat you that way ever again. That I can assure you of."

She stays quiet, almost like she's searching my face for evidence of me telling her the truth.

"First, thank you for the flowers, they were really pretty. Second, I forgive you."

"I don't deserve—"

Mariah holds up her hand before I can continue.

"I understand feeling overwhelmed and not knowing how to process that. With that said, my forgiveness doesn't negate how I felt when you left the room. That doesn't erase the hurt I felt. You abandoned me after signing a contract where you promised to care for me in exchange for my submission to you."

She pierces me directly through my chest, and the worst part? She's one hundred percent correct.

"You're right. I fucked up, full stop. But if you're willing, I'd really like to try to make it up to you and earn back your trust. I also don't want to lose our friendship."

"Can I ask you something?"

"Anything."

"Is it because I didn't do as good of a job as your previous subs?"

Fuck. "No, Mariah. That's not it at all. It was quite the opposite, actually. I hate that you felt even an ounce of rejection and thought for even a moment you weren't good enough. You made me feel more than I've ever felt with a woman. Sex with you was life-altering. I can't go back to a normal life knowing how good it felt to be with you. It was scarier than Ilya's driving."

That gets her to giggle and flash a brief smile my way. Progress. I'll take it.

"I'm doing something scary too. I'm choosing to give you a second chance. Please don't crush me again. I won't survive it."

I pull her hands to my lips, giving them a kiss. "I promise, I will do better. I'll never let you leave here feeling that way again."

"Did you want to teach me something tonight?"

It's now my turn to smile at her. "Hell yeah, I would love to teach you something. How about we focus on oral. You got a little taste last time of me eating that delicious pussy. Would you like to start and enter back into the dom/sub roles now?"

"Yes, I'd like that."

"Get on your knees in front of me." Mariah climbs off the couch and lowers herself to her knees in front of me.

"Be a good girl and take my cock out of my pants." Her delicate hands reach for my belt, undo my button, and pull down my zipper. Every movement she makes is being cataloged in my brain.

"Like this?" She looks up at me while holding my hard-as-steel cock tightly. Causing me to let out a hiss, she squeezes me further.

"Have you ever touched a dick before, Mariah?" Quickly shaking her head back and forth, she continues to stroke me. I get lost not just in the pleasure from her hands, but knowing that I'll forever be the first dick she's seen and touched.

She leans forward, trying to kiss the tip.

"Did I give you permission to put your lips on me?"

"No, you didn't. Can I please kiss it?"

"Yes, lick the tip. Gather all the precum in your mouth." She listens to me so perfectly. "How do I taste, sweetheart?"

"Salty, but I like it."

I run my hand through her gorgeous dark brown waves, gathering a handful of her hair, wrapping it around my fist. I let her take the lead since she's never done this before, but as she starts to put her lips around my dick and take me deeper into the back of her throat, I start to lose my ability to think.

She moves farther down than she intended and lets out a gagging noise. Pulling back, she coughs, and I see spit coating her mouth and chin. I couldn't care less. I love seeing her all messy from trying to please me.

"Your mouth feels so good on my dick. Come sit on my face." I lie back on the couch and help her get into position before pulling her down onto my face. Keeping my hold on her thighs, I let her grind

74

down on my face. She's moving almost instinctively, letting herself feel everything and staying in the moment.

I'm quickly realizing that the taste of her pussy might just be an addiction. I want this every day; I want her every day.

"Don't wait to cum, beautiful. You have permission." As I continue to eat my new favorite meal, she continues to ride my face. She gets her orgasm, but I also want to try sixty-nine. It's something that's just been too intimate to do previously with submissives.

"Spin around so you can put my cock back in your mouth." Eagerly, she follows my instructions, and her warm mouth is soon back on my dick.

We spend however long giving each other endless pleasure. She gets off one more time before I find myself about to cum. "Mariah, if you don't want to swallow, you need to take your mouth off of me. I'm going to cum."

She does the last thing I think she'll do. She starts to suck harder, and I have no choice but to fill her mouth with my seed. I feel her swallow it all, licking my tip clean.

"You're such a good girl for me. So eager to learn. I love how responsive your body is to my touch. I'm proud of you, Mariah."

I help her stand up and lead her to the bathroom myself this time. I turn on the water, filling the large soaking tub. I turn to her and bring her to my chest. Hugging her and having her close to me feels so right. I'm so grateful that she's forgiven me and more importantly, allowed me to continue with our agreement. I'm quickly realizing that I cannot lose her. I think I already knew that, but after the last forty-eight hours, she's woven herself deep inside of my heart.

CHAPTER 8

MARIAH

I spent the last two days feeling so unsettled. I was embarrassed, sad, and hurt. But I think the emotion I felt the most was disappointment. I trusted Niko to take care of me. Trust that normally takes years to build, Niko had in six months, and he threw it all away.

The other side of my emotions after Tuesday had me feeling conflicted. I could tell from the flower delivery yesterday and his texts that he deeply regretted what happened. Sierra said he didn't talk to anyone all day yesterday, which is very unlike him. I received a text again this morning saying that he'd be waiting for me at Rapture.

I waffled back and forth trying to decide whether I'd come here tonight. While I didn't respond to any of his messages because I wanted some space, I am glad he didn't try to call or show up at my apartment. He respected that I put my walls up immediately after leaving on Tuesday. But after work today, I reread his messages and realized that aside from Sierra and her parents, nobody has ever apologized to me if they hurt me.

I understand that puts the bar on the floor, but I was confident he was being genuine in his remorse. He knew he'd fucked up, not just as my dom, but as a man. He didn't treat me the way he promised to. I was glad that he didn't try to shift the blame. He accepted this fell entirely at his feet. I respected that he didn't try to shy away, and he knew almost immediately he didn't do the right thing since he tried to stop me from leaving that night.

I'm pretty sure that he followed me home. I didn't want to ask him, but that'd be more like the Niko I'd grown to know. I hope he didn't come inside though, because when I got home there was a threatening note on my door. That's a problem for another day, after I decide how to proceed with this whole situation between me and Niko.

Ultimately, I chose to come to Rapture tonight for three reasons. One being to at least hear Niko out. He wanted to apologize and I wanted to hear what he had to say. Reason number two: at the end of the day, he's not my boyfriend. We chose a dom/sub arrangement. While he broke that agreement, he isn't necessarily a romantic partner—even if I secretly wish he was. Reason number three: I got horny thinking of the way I felt when he made me orgasm. It was better than anything I'd ever had before, so at the very least, my dick-starved pussy deserved some additional attention. Call me selfish; not sure I care.

I arrive a few minutes late, a purposeful choice that nevertheless stressed me out the entire drive over here. I wanted him to sweat it out a little longer. He deserved to feel a touch of how abandoned I had felt. It was my petty act before allowing him to guide me somewhere private to talk.

His apology in person was just as honest as his texts and the note that came with the flowers were. He looked pretty rough too, like he hadn't been sleeping. Once I learned that it really had nothing to do with me or my performance, it made me feel better. He clearly isn't used to personal connection to his subs, and the way he described how he was feeling so stripped and raw, it resonated with me.

I told him that I forgive him, but made sure to be very clear that I don't give second chances often. He knows he has to rebuild trust with me. He started immediately by showing me lesson two of my sex education.

When he told me to sit on his face, I was super nervous. That's such a vulnerable position. I was afraid to fully sit down, not wanting him to get hurt or be uncomfortable. Niko, however, pulled me down onto him. It was like he was eating my pussy not just for my pleasure, but his own. He suggested we sixty-nine and I was keen to try it.

I'd always wanted to know what it felt like to put a cock in my mouth and have it touch the back of my throat. Let me tell you, Niko delivered. Seeing him up close was exhilarating. I could see every vein that drew my eyes towards the swollen tip of his dick. There was precum leaking out that had my tongue reaching out to lick him clean.

Without saying it, I knew he was still hesitant from what happened earlier this week. But he put on his dom hat as soon as we were done talking about what happened. I was grateful that he took me at my word for forgiveness and didn't hold back during our session.

He carefully asks me, "Was everything okay? Did you like everything?"

"Yes. I think you know I did because I had two orgasms." Niko smirks at my response, clearly proud of his efforts.

The tub is quickly filling, and he reaches for the large glass jar filled with Epsom salts. I can smell a lavender scent coming off the bathwater now. Niko shuts the water off and puts two fluffy towels near the tub.

Climbing into the tub, he holds his hand out for me to join him. I get settled, sitting with my back against his chest. His arms wrap around me, and for the first time in my life, I feel cherished.

I know that sounds odd, considering we've been intimate, but this feels like he genuinely cares about my well-being beyond just as a friend. I know that he's contractually obligated, but part of me enjoys this. I've never had a man take care of me this way.

"Do you have a hair tie so I can put your hair up?"

I pull one off my wrist and hold it out for him. He takes the hair tie, and I feel him gently gather my hair and put the tie around it so my hair can stay dry in the tub.

"I'm grateful that you forgave me. I know that I fucked up. I promise to make sure you never feel the way you did when you left here on Tuesday ever again. I swear, Mariah, I've never acted that way and I won't again because you mean so much to me. I felt so sick to my stomach, I didn't even talk to anyone the past couple of days."

"I know. Sierra told me. Let's move on from this and keep rebuilding the trust, okay?"

"Agreed." And he pulls me back against him tightly and kisses my shoulder.

We continue to cuddle in the water until it's room temperature. After we dry off, he helps me get dressed again. Holding my hand, he leads me to the lobby. "Can I drive you home?"

"Yeah, that'd be great, actually," I respond with a smile, grateful that I can skip Ubering home.

He opens the passenger door on his SUV, which is parked near the door of Rapture. After I'm settled in the car, he closes the door to walk over to his side. I've been in his car before, but tonight specifically, I notice how much it smells like Niko.

He pulls away from the curb and takes the short drive to my apartment. While I don't have a car, my building always has spots available in front. He parks and says, "Wait for me to get your door, please."

Unbuckling my seat belt, I wait for him to open my door and hold his hand out for me to get out of his car. I grab my purse to pull out my keys as we walk up to the door. Niko stays close as we enter the elevator.

"I know we normally would meet next on Saturday, but I don't think I can wait that long to have you back with me, Mariah. Can we meet tomorrow?"

"Yeah, we can meet tomorrow. That's fine. Same time?" The elevator opens to my floor and we walk towards my door.

"If that works for you, I'll be there at seven."

As we approach my door, my stomach sinks. There's another note. Who the fuck is doing this?

I quickly yank it down and try to shove it into my purse. Niko looks puzzled, but doesn't ask me about it. He leans in to give me a kiss, which I happily return. I unlock the door and hear him leave as I flip the lock back into place.

Trying to steady my breathing, I grab the note from my purse.

> *You will regret going down this path. Leave it alone, Mariah.*

To say I'm scared is an understatement. The calls were a nuisance, but these notes, particularly so close together, have me officially freaked out. Whoever this is, they know where I live, and that's terrifying. None of the messages make any sense and they're never the same.

I pull out my phone to text Sierra to see if she wants to hang out on Saturday.

> Want to maybe do lunch or something on Saturday?

She's already typing a response before I can close out of my messaging app.

> Sierra: Yes. Come over here. We can watch a movie and have lunch. Just come whenever!

> Sounds good! How are you feeling, mama?

> Sierra: I'm doing okay. Tired AF but the girls are so sweet with trying to help me out.

> They're gonna be such good big sisters for baby Kira! I'll see you Saturday!

While I try to go to sleep, I think of how much my circle has grown the past year. I never thought I'd have anyone get close to me besides Sierra. After everything that my mom put me through, I never wanted to have a bigger group around me. My mom actively tried to make my life hell. From verbal to sometimes physical abuse, I struggled so much to hide my home life from everyone. I got used to hiding and still find comfort in the quiet versus loud places.

Waking up to my alarm blaring next to me, I'm a little slow to get out of bed. Though, as of the last couple of months, Fridays have become my favorite day of the week. Today will be a good one. I've been having calls with Juan for the past several Fridays, and then Niko switched our days so I'll end my day getting orgasms. Not a bad way to start the weekend.

After getting ready for work and making a morning cup of coffee, I settle at my desk to get started with my day. There's a few onboarding meetings with clients that go well and I'm also able to set up some interviews with nannies for those new families. Before I know it, my phone rings with Juan's name appearing on the screen.

"Hey, Juan! Happy Friday."

"Sis, how's your week been?"

"Pretty good. I've just been working. I'll be hanging out with my friend tomorrow, which I'm excited about. She's pregnant, so I want to start to plan her baby shower."

"You've mentioned that. How exciting for her. Do they know what they're having?"

"A baby girl. They're planning to name her Kira."

"That's a precious name. I hope she's having a good pregnancy."

"Thanks. So far so good. I know she's been tired. Anyways, have any plans for this weekend?"

"I wanted to talk to you about that, actually. Do you have plans for Sunday?"

"No, I'm free. What's up?"

I can hear his hesitancy before he answers. "I was thinking, if you're interested, we can have lunch somewhere. Maybe with Dad?"

I'm stunned. I thought when this moment came I'd be really nervous, but now that it's here, I'm excited and very optimistic.

"I think I'd like that. Are you sure he'd want to meet me?"

"Sierra, I promise you that he'll be thrilled. My mom will be just as excited. I've told you before, we all knew that my dad has always wondered if he had another child. The whole family will be ecstatic."

"Have you told him about me yet?"

"I was planning to do that tomorrow, if you agreed to lunch on Sunday."

"Okay, yeah, I think it'd be nice to meet you all. Have a place in mind?"

"Ever been to The Langham? They do a delicious lunch."

I'm happy that he suggested somewhere public. I know that they're my family, but I've never met them.

"That'd be nice. Does one o'clock sound good?"

"Sure. I'll make the reservation after we get off the phone." Juan sounds really enthusiastic about setting up our first meeting.

We keep talking for another half hour while I make my lunch, tossing together a quick salad. We hang up just as I start to eat and log back on from my break.

As I'm working, I think about asking Misha if he can send someone with me to meet my family on Sunday. Maybe Ilya? I just want to be safe, especially with the phone calls and notes. I need to be careful. I'm not like Sierra—I can't just go fight a man or shoot him. I can do basic self-defense, thanks to her dad, but that's about it.

I can't help but feel like I'm being watched ever since the notes started arriving. Whoever is threatening me, they know where I live. I should probably bring it up to Misha. I've been debating it for the last couple of weeks, but the escalation to my door is too much. He says he still owes me for saving Alexandra, which he definitely doesn't, but I won't look that gift horse in the mouth. I decide to cash in on that I-owe-you and see if he can somehow find out who's following me.

CHAPTER 9

NIKO

"Uncle Niko, are you sure that this is good enough to implement?" Tati asks, sitting next to me in Sam's office at Fedorov Industries. Over the last few months since she started working with me for her training, Misha has let me take her out of school for a half day every other week to bring her down to the offices to get her feet wet in some of the corporate aspects.

Unlike her training with Toly, which could be done after school since it's largely remote, Tati's training with me sometimes does need to take place during normal office hours. This setup allows her to meet with additional people and get to participate in some of the meetings that pertain to her training directly. Currently, she's telling Sam and me about her tentative plan for updating inventory protocols before she proceeds with trying to implement it.

Answering her question for me, Sam responds, "Tati, this is really good. You took the week to come up with some good ideas here. I think what you should do next is research best practices on what should be included on the spreadsheets and create a draft. We can try to do a small dry run of it after Toly's team sets up the FTP."

I notice she sits up a little taller when my friend gives her positive feedback. I know Sam doesn't hand out empty compliments—he thinks her work is valuable and needed. Tati's known Sam her whole life and is aware that he'd never bullshit her if he didn't like what she'd suggested.

"Okay, that makes sense. I'll work on that for next week. I also had a question about the line item that was for community outreach?"

We both nod, urging her to ask her question.

"Are there any organizations that work in the arts? I know that it'd be nice for Alexandra to know that we are sponsoring a local art club or scholarships to art school? Not sure if I can have any say in that, but I think it'd be nice for her to know that we do that." I put my hand on her knee, proudly giving her a smile.

"I think that'd be a really nice gesture. We can come up with a short list of organizations and go from there." I'm not her father, but after Elena passed, I moved in with Misha and the girls to help them in the initial wake of her death. I grew very close to my nieces, and even after I moved out I still maintained that relationship with them.

We keep moving the meeting along, covering everything that Sam needed to discuss with me. After another hour, I walk with Tati down

86

to the parking garage. I open the passenger door for her, and she wraps her arms around my waist in a hug. We're an affectionate family, but needing to make sure she's okay, I ask, "Everything alright, honey?"

"Yeah, just really grateful that you all are training me. I like getting to work with you and Sam."

I smile and kiss the top of her head. She's tall, probably close to five and a half feet already at only thirteen. She'll be a formidable Pakhan one day. I can't wait to see how my brother acts when he retires in favor of his daughter. I'm beyond confident that she'll be worthy of the role when the time comes.

"Of course. You're doing really well. We're all incredibly proud of you."

She hops into the car and I shut the door of my luxury SUV. Once I get settled, I back out of the spot and head towards Misha's house to drop her off. I'll have just enough time after to make my way to meet Mariah at Rapture. Tati and I make small talk about her schoolwork and she tells me tryouts for spring soccer are coming up after winter break.

As we pull up to the house, Ilya opens the gate for my car. I wave to him and notice Tati blushing a little as we move up the long driveway. Not wanting to embarrass her, I file that away to bring up later. I'm guessing she knows that I noticed her response to Ilya, so she quickly hops out of the car, shouting good night over her shoulder as she walks briskly into the house. I laugh because I know Misha's head will explode. Ilya's a good kid though; he knows better than to even entertain Tati. He's also six years older than her.

Making my way back to the road, I turn my thoughts to the temptress I can't get enough of. I couldn't wait until tomorrow to have her, so last night, rescheduling our meeting made so much sense in my head. Now that she's had a few days to heal after her first time, I want to introduce some of the toys that I've been dreaming about using with her.

She's so responsive to my touch. It's beautiful to watch her cum, and tonight I'll be able to better exert my dominance now that she's had basic oral and penetrative sex. We can graduate to some entry-level toys and restraints. Knowing exactly what I have in mind, I'm grateful that traffic and lights are on my side tonight.

Parking in my usual spot, I nod to the two guards standing outside of Rapture. Making my way inside, I wave to Iris and let her know I'll be back in a few minutes to get Mariah. I head straight to the room I reserved for tonight. There's a dresser in each room that has condoms, but the top drawer tonight is filled with the toys I requested Iris bring in after I formulated my plan for tonight.

Setting out the red silk ties on the top of the dresser, I turn back to the drawer to find the vibrator. Feeling good about what's going to happen tonight, I get into my role of dominant and go wait for Mariah in the lobby. On my way back, I walk through the playroom and decide that I want to start here. She seemed to enjoy watching that first night, but let her nerves distract her. I want to see her embrace that.

I still have some leftover guilt over how Tuesday went down, but I'm working on letting those deeper feelings just sit to the side. I want to experience this with her so badly, because for me, all of this is a first too. For the first time, I want more. For the first time, I want to have a woman, specifically Mariah, by my side as more than a submissive or a hidden part of my life. If I could, I'd let the world know she belongs to me.

Standing off to the side, I see the moment she crests the staircase and my jaw drops. She walks in wearing a skintight dress, highlighting her figure. I walk right up to her, I whisper in her ear, "Fuck, Mariah. You came to play tonight, didn't you?"

I hear her breathing stutter before she squeaks out, "Yes. I've had this dress for a while, but never was confident enough to wear it." My heart soars, hoping that means she feels confident with me. After everything, that would mean so much to me. I'm glad I still make her comfortable and feel safe enough to wear something that she normally wouldn't wear.

Adjusting my cock, which is now hard from seeing her walking into the lobby, I lead her into the playroom, which has gotten busy. I see an available couch that faces the open room—it'll give us a good view of the stage area. She's looking at me, showing some nerves but trying to seem unbothered for my sake.

"Are you okay?" I rub my hand up and down her back.

"Yeah, I'm good. Promise." She's distracted, but I don't think it has anything to do with being here. With our dynamic, I can only take what she says at face value. I have to trust that she'll tell me if she's uncomfortable.

After I sit down on the couch, I pull her onto my lap. I know she immediately feels my erection pressing against her ass. As she starts to look around the playroom, her eyes stop at one group. She looks back at me, making sure she's not just seeing things. I give her a nod and a smile. She turns back to keep watching. The group she's got her eye on? Well, it's Sam with a woman and another man. The two men have their woman restrained on a St. Andrew's cross and each man has begun to suck on her breasts. Their hands are both stroking her pussy. The woman's eyes close as she gets close to orgasming for Sam and their third.

Mariah's mouth is open as she continues to watch. Her thighs tighten, and I whisper into her ear, "Are you wet, baby? Does watching my best friend make another woman cum get you off?" The flush that crawls up her neck is immediate. I know this is all new to her, but she's read really spicy and dark romance books for years, so the concepts and kinks aren't shocking to her, but seeing them in real life versus on-page has to be jarring.

Continuing to murmur in her ear, I say, "Just so you know, I don't share. Don't get yourself too worked up, sweetheart."

"Yes, sir." That's the first time she's said that to me, and it has me bolting up from the couch with her still in my arms. I carry her to the room I was preparing earlier. I toss her onto the bed. Going back to the door, I flip the lock and grab the silk ties from the dresser. As I turn back to face her, I see she's taken off all of her clothes.

"Checking in, Mariah. What color?"

"Green. Definitely green."

I smile at her, happy that she's excited about this new lesson. "That's my good girl. I'm going to tie your hands above your head, okay?"

She nods and I work the ties through the headboard, careful to make my knots, ensuring they won't hurt her.

"Everything feel good?"

"Yes, they're okay."

"I'm gonna spread those thighs now and tie you open around each of your ankles."

"Yes, please."

I work to get her spread open for me. When I'm done, I admire my work. "You're mine. You know that, right? You're mine and only mine." When I hear the words leave my mouth, it scares me how much I mean them. If the opportunity to make that true outside of these four walls ever came up, I'd make her mine for real.

Getting out of my head, I stare at her. She looks fucking hot tied up, waiting for me to continue. I go back to the dresser to grab the vibrator. Flicking it on, I crawl onto the bed to join her.

"You've used something like this before right, sweetheart?" I wave the toy around.

"Yes, I have a couple at home."

I run the toy through the wetness that's gathered near her vagina. Once I'm satisfied the vibrator has enough of her wetness to glide over her clit, I bring it up and know the moment it hits the right spot for her. She flexes her hands into fists and her head rolls to the side. Adjusting my position so I'm able to get my mouth onto her tits, I latch on to one of her nipples and suck.

Continuing to move the vibrator around her clit, I feel her inching closer and closer to an orgasm. Letting go of her breast, I also pull the vibrator away.

"Hey! What are you doing? I was almost there!" Good, she's frustrated.

"I didn't give you permission to cum. I'm in charge of all of your orgasms, remember? Now be a good little submissive and know that I'll ensure you get everything you need."

Like a little brat, she sassily responds, "You better."

Turning off the vibrator, I put it back onto a towel sitting on the dresser top. I strip out of all my clothes and grab a condom. Not ready to put it on, I stroke my cock a few times to take some of the edge off. I see her eyes laser focused on what my hands are doing.

"You want my cock, don't you?"

She nods her head. "Yes, sir. Please, can I have your cock now?"

"Not yet. I need to taste this delicious pussy for a minute first."

Putting the condom next to her hip, I settle between her still spread open thighs. There's a small wet stain on the sheets from where she's dripped. As if my dick needed to get any harder. My mouth finds her hardened clit and gives it some suction. I gently bring two fingers inside of her and curl them back towards me. I can't believe that when I set up this schedule, I thought I could go more than twenty-four hours without tasting her.

Her walls start to clench my fingers and I pull them out immediately, giving her pussy a light tap. She instantly grows more frustrated that I haven't let her cum yet. "Checking in. What color?"

"Still green, but if you don't let me get an orgasm soon, it might not even be my fault if I can't stop it."

"Yes, it will. You don't want to get punished, do you? Bad girls don't get my cock."

"I'll be good, I swear. You're the one in charge, I promise." I laugh out loud. She is really on edge, and it's so fucking hot.

I tear open the condom, then roll it down my shaft before letting the wrapper fall to the floor. On my knees, I reach over her head and release the restraints. I quickly move to her ankles, and I let those go too.

"Hands and knees, now."

She moves so fast, following my instructions like the eager sub she is. Her ass is in the air, and I can't help but stare at the view. She looks incredible like this.

"You okay if I go a little rougher this time?" I need to make sure she's good before I start.

"Yes. Please, Nikolai. Please, fuck me." Hearing her say my full name has my hips moving on instinct to thrust full tilt inside of her tight pussy. The pussy that's only felt my cock. *And will only ever feel my cock,* I say to myself.

I grab a hold of her hips and use the extra leverage to get deep thrusts. I never want these three months to end. "You feel so fucking good, Mariah. Your pussy is squeezing my dick." I smack her ass, and when the slight redness appears in the shape of my handprint, I get off on seeing my marks on her. I give her another spanking, and another. She is moaning through the sting each time my hand meets her flesh.

"Give me your arms. Now."

Obediently, she brings her arms behind her back and I secure them with my right hand, while my left finds its way to her head and pushes down.

"You're such a good cock slut, aren't you? You play a meek little virgin, but you're a vixen, aren't you? You've got me falling to my knees. I'm supposed to be your dom, but I'd crawl to you if you asked."

Her hands wrap around my wrist that's been holding her hands at the base of her spine. She's moaning my name like it's a prayer.

"Cum for me, Mariah. Cum right fucking now. Cum on my cock." After nearly twenty-five minutes of edging, she finally gets her release. I can only last a few more thrusts before I succumb to my own orgasm.

Continuing some light movements of my hips to let her ride out the rest of her pleasure, I let her arms go then slowly pull out.

Mariah flips onto her back and looks at me with a smile.

I cheekily ask her, "Did you enjoy yourself?"

"Immensely. That was really fun."

"Yeah? The degradation was okay?"

"Yes. It wasn't nasty; it was hot, actually."

I'm glad she's enjoying this next step. I remove the condom and toss it into the trash, along with the wrapper I dropped earlier.

"Let's jump in the shower, yeah?" She follows me into the shower and I hold her close. I slowly clean her off, and when we get out, I ask her, "Can I brush your hair for you?"

She hands me the large-tooth comb that she has in her purse. I gently make my way through her now-wet hair. "You're beautiful, you know that?" I comment quietly while maintaining my eye contact with her in the mirror. She doesn't say anything, but I also didn't expect her to. I know she didn't get treated kindly while growing up. I want to change that.

Once we're dressed again, I ask her if I can drive her home again and she accepts. We walk out to my car and make the short drive to her condo. Pulling into the same spot as last night, I follow her inside and into the elevator.

"Will you be at Misha's tomorrow?" she asks.

"Yeah, most of the day. I'll be working on some stuff with Tati and catching up on inventory."

"I'll probably see you then. Sierra and I are going to hang out. I need to start planning her baby shower, too. Hopefully I can get that moving."

"I know you'll make it incredibly special for her, so try not to stress too much about it."

"Thanks. I can't wait to be a fun auntie."

"Having nieces is the best."

When the elevator doors open, she begins to walk very quickly. There's another note taped to her door.

"Who's that from?"

"N-nobody. Thanks for the ride." She answers too quickly and moves fast to unlock the door. She slides in, and through the now-closed door, she tells me to have a good night.

Deciding tonight wouldn't be the best time to bring it up, I head back to my car and drive through Friday-night Chicago traffic to get over to my place in Lakeshore East. My building has stunning views of the lake, but with the sun setting so early in December, I don't see much as the elevator climbs to mine and Toly's floor. The elevator was designed to face outward, so you have a view while climbing the floors.

"Evening Mr. Fedorov." The guards on duty greet me as I open the door to my place.

"Night, boys." I nod my thanks.

Rasputin comes to the door to greet me. He's such a happy pup. I adopted him when I moved out of Misha's place three years ago. During the summers, he and I love to go on long runs along Lakefront Trail to the beach. If we go early enough in the morning, I'll let him dig a few holes in the sand before I fill them back in.

I pour myself a glass of vodka, then I turn on the heater outside on my balcony. Rasputin follows me outside and jumps onto the couch that I keep out here year-round. I look out over the lake. Navy Pier is to the left of my building, but I can see the Ferris wheel clear as day, full of tourists enjoying the city. I start to let my mind wander.

How the fuck did I end up with the most forbidden woman as my submissive? I wish I could have her like a normal boyfriend. Never been one before, but for her I'd try, I really would. She consumes my every thought. She's become a huge part of my life and I wish there was a way to see if she'd ever want more without spooking her. Because if she said no, I wouldn't keep pushing, I'd accept that. But it's the not knowing that keeps a flicker of hope alive in the depths of my brain.

I know she for sure doesn't want kids. I've thought about this piece a lot. I was never fixated on having my own children. If it were to happen, great, but if not, also great. I love having my nieces and I'm sure the rest of my family will also eventually have children, so it's not like I'd never get baby snuggles. Turning to my dog, I say, "What do you think? I bet you'd enjoy being an only child, huh?" He lifts his head and gives me a short bark.

So what if I spoil my dog? I'm a millennial; it's what we do. I might be a killer, but I have a coffee addiction, no kids, and a rescue dog. I spend a little more time outside before finishing off my drink. I check to see when Rasputin was last taken out. The chart says ten, so he's fine for the night.

I head to my bedroom, and not for the first time since we met, I fall asleep wishing Mariah was next to me.

Chapter 10

Mariah

After I basically shut my front door in Niko's face, I spend the next few hours vacillating between hyperventilating with anxiety and being thoroughly pissed that someone feels the need to threaten me.

Like, for real, why me? I live the quietest life I can. I have one really good friend, a job that is remote, and a half brother I've only ever talked to on the phone. I live a fairly isolated life, one I'm content with.

Then I'm hit with the same realization that I had earlier this week. My circle has grown so much this year. I have more people who care about me than I've ever had. Niko included.

These are the thoughts that have offered me comfort since I locked away the note with the others. Now, I'm in bed, trying to calm down as much as possible, when I make a rash decision to stay quiet and not tell Misha after all.

I need to protect Sierra at all costs. She's given me so much in this life. I can't stress her out with a mess that's likely of my own making. How is that true? I'm not really sure, but lying awake at two in the morning has me rethinking my whole plan with Misha later today.

I'll still be asking him for a guard to come to Sunday brunch with Juan, but I'm firm in my decision to not bring this to him—yet. If there's another incident, I'll tell him, but for now I want to bury my head a little longer.

I'm scared and freaked out. However, I'm feeling more protective of my friend, who'll without a doubt try to insert herself into helping fight this stalker. Not fully sure if this can be classified as a stalker, but it feels like it should be. I don't want to expose her to that stress.

I continue rolling around in my bed like a damn rotisserie chicken before finally getting a few hours of sleep. I'm grateful as hell that it's a Saturday, so I don't have any work today, and I sleep in pretty late. After getting up and taking the laziest shower ever, I finish getting ready so that I can head over to Sierra's.

December in Chicago can mean literally anything weather-wise. Today, it's upper forties and sunny. It actually feels quite nice, so I decide to at least walk a part of the way and enjoy the sun. After twenty minutes and a stop at a coffee shop, I hop into a waiting Uber to take me the rest of the way.

As always, Ilya is manning the gate and lets me in straight away once I get out of the car. He works really hard for the family and their trust in him is evident through his position in their organization.

I don't even make it up the stairs to the front door before it swings open and Sierra's launching herself at me in a big hug, although it's getting a bit tight with her growing bump between us.

98

"Wow, your bump really popped!" I say with a wide smile. I can't help but be happy for my friend. She's going to be such an amazing mom. Sierra grabs my hand and lays it over her belly. I feel the kicks from Kira under my hand.

"She's been moving so much, I swear she thinks it's always time to party." Sierra leads us to the dining room where Irina, Tati, and Alexandra are waiting to eat with us. I love getting to come over here and spend time with these ladies.

As I pull my chair out, Niko's mom, Anastasia, walks in carrying a tray of little sandwiches. As she sets the tray down, she quickly comes over to give me a hug. "So good to see you, Mariah. How have you been, dorogaya?"

I learned a few months ago that she's calling me darling. Irina called me that the first few times I came here. When I asked what it meant, she said it's just a term of endearment. To them it might mean nothing, but to me, it feels like I belong.

"Hi, Anastasia. Everything's been great. Thanks for having me." I really hate lying to everyone when they ask me how I'm doing.

"This is Sierra and Misha's house." She laughs. I love her dry humor; it reminds me a lot of Niko. "But, yes, I'm glad you could join us."

We talk about everything from Sierra's pregnancy to the girls' winter break, holiday planning, and lastly Sierra's baby shower.

It's so fun getting to be around them, and it makes me feel guilty that I'm hiding a few rather big secrets. Between my agreement with Niko and the stalker situation, I've never hidden so much from Sierra. Seeing her happy resolves my decision to stay quiet—for now.

"Okay, girls, help me clear the table," I say to Tati and Alexandra as I push my chair back, grabbing mine and Sierra's plates. The three of us work quickly to clear the table and put all the dishes in the dishwasher. We created a line to wash the platters and whatever else couldn't fit into the dishwasher.

Sierra sat at the kitchen island while we finished up with the dishes and a grateful Irina pulled out a batch of cookies she'd made earlier this morning for us to enjoy. I swipe a couple of them, and immediately take a bite. I can taste the white chocolate chips and it's easily one of the best cookies I've had. Irina never misses the mark on her baking or cooking.

"Irina, these are delicious. Where'd you get the recipe?" I hope it's not a family secret because I'd love to make these during my holiday baking.

"Oh, I actually found it a few years ago in a magazine. I can text you the recipe, if you want."

"Yes, please. I'd love to make these in a couple weeks with the rest of my Christmas cookies."

The girls head out to do their own thing, and eventually Sierra and I wind up in the family room, huddled on the couch with soft blankets, watching a Netflix Christmas movie. Halfway through the movie, I see that Sierra's fallen asleep. Just as I go to wake her up, her eyes fly open and she sprints—well, as fast as a six-month-pregnant woman can sprint—to the bathroom.

Coming back, she's rubbing her hand over the bump. "Apparently, my bladder is already in danger," she says, laughing.

Taking this as the best time to talk about my family stuff, I say to her, "Hey, I have a favor I want to ask Misha. Will you come with me?"

She turns very serious. "Is everything okay?"

Lying through my teeth, I say, "Yeah, I just have some news, and I'd like his help with something, if it's okay?"

"Of course. Let's go; he should be in his office."

Together, we walk down to the office wing of the house. Passing each of the offices, some of the doors are open, including Niko's. I see him alone in his office, sitting behind his desk, laser focused on whatever's on his screen.

We walk into Misha's office and Sierra saunters straight to him. He smiles wide and takes off his glasses. He pulls my friend onto his lap, and she tries to stand up. "Misha, I'm too big."

"Never, zhena. You're carrying my baby and look absolutely stunning." His lips reach her cheek in a chaste kiss. "What are you ladies up to today?"

"We were just talking and watching a movie. I fell asleep, only to be woken up by your daughter doing a dance on my bladder. But Mariah wanted to ask for a favor." My friend turns to look at me.

I move closer to his desk and sit down in one of the chairs across from him and Sierra. I realize how nervous I am. While I've gotten better at asking for help, mainly thanks to my friend just inserting herself where required so I don't have to ask, it isn't something that comes easy.

"I should probably start at the beginning. I'm not sure how much Sierra's told you about my family life when I was younger. I didn't know who my father was, but over the summer, I took a DNA test for one of those websites. I was lucky enough to get a twenty-five percent paternal match—a half brother. One I share with my father.

"I wasn't sure if I'd reach out or not, but earlier in the fall I decided to message him. After a few weeks, Juan and I moved to phone calls

101

every Friday during our lunch hour. It's been really great getting to know him, and learning about my father has been a real joy for me. We have been wanting to meet in person and Juan suggested tomorrow at The Langham. It's not that I don't trust Juan or our dad, but I've never met either of them. I was hoping you'd maybe let me borrow a guard or soldier to come with me?

"I've gotten more comfortable with your family, but these are two men I've never met. I'd feel safer if I had someone with me." Looking down at my hands, I say, "I still don't feel safe around strangers and it'd mean a lot to me if you could send someone with me."

"I'll do it, I'll go with her," a voice behind me announces. I don't need to turn around to know exactly who is behind me. But what I am unclear on is why Niko would volunteer for an errand like this.

"Oh, no, that's okay. Ilya would be fine."

"I'm more than happy to go with you, Mariah. I don't have plans tomorrow." Niko doesn't even phrase it like there's a question of whether he'll be the one to go with me tomorrow.

"Mariah, if you're worried about safety, I'd prefer one of my brothers or cousins went with you versus one of the guards," Misha insists.

"Are you sure?" I ask.

"I think Niko going with you makes the most sense." He nods towards his brother in approval. The Pakhan has spoken, but he doesn't know that he's just agreed to letting my sex teacher/dom be my escort when I meet my brother and bio-dad for the first time. What a fucking sentence that is.

"Okay, now that's all figured out, I think Irina is waiting on us to decorate cookies. Let's go, everyone." Sierra hops—well slowly gets up—from her husband's lap to lead us all to the dining room. Irina and Anastasia have a bunch of different colored icings and dozens of cookies set out on the table. Toly and the girls follow us in and immediately grab seats to start icing their cookies.

We all—and I mean all of the Fedorovs, including Maxim—spend the afternoon decorating Christmas cookies. I have so much fun. Spending this time with them does more for my soul than therapy ever did. I feel like I belong with them. Which is odd, because a group of six-foot-plus muscly tattooed men would've had me on edge a year ago, but these men have never made me feel like an outsider.

Maxim comes over to me and asks how I'm doing, saying that Misha told him about my father. "You know that we'll keep you safe, right?"

"I do. And you have no idea how good that feels. Thank you."

He pulls me in for a hug before returning to help his granddaughters.

I feel Niko's eyes on me, and as I look up, he's sitting there staring at me. He motions with his head for me to go out to the hallway.

Quietly, he asks me, "What do you know about your brother?"

"Juan is twenty-four and he has a degree in chemistry from UCLA. He works with our dad. Why?"

"Why didn't you tell any of us?"

"I wanted to learn about him without background checks and making a big deal out of it. It felt like less pressure this way, in case it didn't work out."

"What do you mean?"

"Well, like, what if I was going to ruin my dad's marriage, or he didn't want to meet me? Worse, what if Juan thought I was too weird, or whatever, to tell our dad about me?"

"And you're confident he doesn't think those things?"

I laugh. "Well, apparently my dad always wondered why my mom took off. They had a broken condom during one of their last times together and he always feared that he might've had a child he never knew. Turns out I wasn't a dirty secret—or, not the possibility of me, anyways. Juan says his mom would love to meet me too. So yeah, I feel like there's no danger of harming anyone by meeting with them."

He gives me a hug, kissing my head. I love the way he makes me feel when his arms are wrapped around me, but I back away because we said no affection outside of Rapture, no matter how nice it feels.

Thrown off by me pulling away, he steers the conversation back to the reason he's helping me. "What time did Juan say to meet for lunch?"

"Reservation was at one o'clock."

"I'll pick you up at a quarter past noon, okay? That way, we'll be a little early."

I smile because he's picked up on my need to be early to everything.

"I'd appreciate that. And thank you for offering to come with me tomorrow."

I head back to the dining room and place the cookies that I decorated into a box that Irina hands me. I go around and say goodbye to everyone, then Misha tells me that Ilya will drive me home since he gets off now. Irina also hands me a box of cookies for him.

I meet my ride home outside. We jump into his car and I hand Ilya the box of cookies.

"Did Irina make these? Her sugar cookies are always top tier."

"Yep, she did. That woman really is an amazing cook."

He drives towards my place and shares some of his childhood with me. "She is. I remember my dad bringing home tins of cookies each year baked by her. My father was one of Maxim's brigadiers, so Irina used to bake them all cookies as a treat during the holidays. They were the highlight of our Christmas desserts because, despite how much I love my mom, she can't bake or cook. So whatever Irina sent home with my dad was usually what I set out for Santa."

This kid is so funny. He talks like his childhood was decades ago, but he likely was still doing it eight or nine years ago.

Once he drops me off, I head up to my place and put on some comfy clothes before I grab my latest spicy book. Just as I sit down, my phone starts to ring. I see it's Juan.

"Hey, how's it going? Are we still on for tomorrow?"

"Of course. I just was calling to let you know that I made the reservations and I'll be telling our dad tonight. I'm actually driving over there now."

"I hope it goes okay. You can text me if he changes his mind. I won't be hurt." Yes, I would be, but I don't want to put pressure on him.

"Yes, you would be, Sis. But that's not going to happen. I promise, he'll be so excited. I'll see you tomorrow, okay?"

"Yes. Tomorrow. Can't wait."

He hangs up and I read until it's time to get ready for bed. For the first time all week, I fall asleep to something other than thoughts of my stalker. I get to meet my dad tomorrow. I've waited my whole life for this moment and I hope it goes smoothly.

CHAPTER 11
JUAN ALVAREZ

I hang up with my sister Mariah as I pull up to my parents' house in Oak Park. As I drive towards the house I grew up in, I'm excited to see that it has been decorated for Christmas. The lights cover the trees in the front yard and the twelve-foot Christmas tree can be seen in the windows. Controversial, but my mom insists on using colored lights. She and my dad have argued over that my entire life. Not shocking—my mom wins every year.

This house is incredibly special to me. It's full of childhood memories, including ones with Bianca, my younger sister who died almost ten years ago. Her death still haunts me each and every day. She was only ten years old when she was killed by a stray bullet in a drive-by shooting. My whole family was in the car, and there was nothing we could do to save her. Watching my sister die will forever be seared into my memory.

My father spent three months after her murder hunting down her killers. It was the first time I joined him in torturing our enemies. I might've only been fifteen, but I was determined to hurt those responsible for killing my sister. They deserved everything that happened to them.

My mother didn't smile again until I was graduating high school. We've slowly healed from Bianca's loss, which is what started my search for my potential sibling. Not that we could ever replace Bianca, but if there was someone else who was a part of this family, I wanted to find them. I took the DNA test almost two years ago and to be honest, never thought I'd find anyone.

When I got the notification that I had a match for a paternal half sister, I was so fucking happy. I waited for weeks for her to reach out. I didn't want to spook her by messaging her first. When I got that initial message from Mariah, I wanted to run and tell my parents. But I couldn't let them be heartbroken if she was just after money or didn't want to have a relationship with us moving forward.

So over the past few months, every time I've got to text or call Mariah, I've had a pinch-me moment. I know she's more than willing to have a relationship with us and I can proudly say that I have an older sister. She's definitely shy, and I'm not sure how my dad will handle learning about her childhood, but getting to meet her tomorrow will be a Christmas gift my parents will never forget.

Getting out of my car, I wave to the guards who watch over my parents' house. Before I can get to the front door, my mom pulls it open and leans against the doorframe, smiling at me, waiting for me with open arms. Getting a hug from Camila Alvarez will make anything better. Sick? Sad? Happy? Doesn't matter, her hugs fix everything. I might be a twenty-four-year-old cartel heir, but I'll never turn down my mother's affection.

I really do think I have the best mom in the world. She knew what she was getting into when she married my dad, the leader of the Alvarez Cartel. My whole family is involved in the organization. My

Tio Jorge handles operations for our family in Mexico. He's my dad's younger brother and the smartest man I've ever met. He would help me over Skype with math homework growing up.

I mainly handle his role here in the US and Canada. Working directly under my dad, Felipe, I've started to learn my future role as el Jefe of our family.

"Hola, Mama. I need to talk to you and Papa. Where's he at?"

"In his office. Is everything okay?"

"Yes, but I have something important to tell you both."

She takes my hand and walks with me down the hallway to where my dad is sitting behind his desk. He has the fireplace lit and a book in his hand that he looks up from as we walk in. "Juan, I didn't think you'd be stopping by today. You okay?"

"Yeah, I have some news that I've been wanting to tell you about."

My dad nods for me to continue.

"I took a DNA test last summer and didn't hear anything until July of this year. Dad, I got a match. I have a half sister."

Both of my parents are shocked. My mom brings her hand to her face and I see a tear drip down her cheek.

"What do you mean?" my dad asks.

"I'll start from the beginning. After I got the notification of a match, I waited a couple of weeks and I got a message from her. Her name is Mariah. She's twenty-eight, which fits your timeline, Papa. We started to text, and more recently have started having weekly phone calls. She lives here in the city and works as a coordinator for a high-end nanny agency."

I pause to really look at my parents. My dad is crying now, too. I've seen him cry a few times in my life, but never because he was happy.

"I always wondered if someone was out there. Sometimes I'd think about looking for them, but I had nothing to go on."

"I know. I thought this would be an easy way to get started without dedicating any resources or manpower to a search."

"How is she? Mariah, you said, right?"

"Yeah her name's Mariah. And she's okay. She hasn't talked to her mom in over twelve years. She hasn't told me too much, but she's told me that her childhood wasn't very good." I wince because I know that will hurt my dad. He can't stand when one of his children is hurt or struggling.

"Twelve years? She would've only been sixteen. Why was a minor left alone?" He's getting angry on her behalf, but I let him know that's all I know.

"She's pretty untrusting of strangers. I've been talking with her for about three months and she's only recently opened up a little about her childhood. I know she lived with her friend and her friend's parents after her mom left."

I know my dad is feeling extremely guilty. "I hate that she grew up that way."

My mom walks over to him and gives him a hug.

"Would you like to meet her?" I ask them both.

My dad is quick with his response. "Of course. Yes, I want to meet mija. When can we get that setup, Juan?"

I smile, because I knew they'd both be excited and anxious, which is why I held off telling them until the night before so they didn't have to wait too long. "We'll be having lunch with her at one p.m. tomorrow at The Langham."

My dad gets up and comes to give me a hug. "Gracias, mijo. Thank you for finding her. I love you so much."

"Love you too, Papa." I return his hug and my mom joins us in our embrace. "She has a lot of trust issues, so just remember to tread carefully tomorrow, okay?"

Shaking his head, my dad says, "Yes, I can imagine that Sylvia didn't make for the best mother figure. Anything else you can tell me about Mariah?"

"Yeah. She's really close to her friend from childhood still. The friend recently got married and is expecting a baby so she's been excited about that lately."

"I'm glad she's not been alone this whole time."

My mom looks to me and asks, "Want to stay for dinner? It's just about ready."

"Yeah, that'd be nice, I haven't eaten yet."

I pull out my phone and text Mariah.

> I just told Dad. Him and my mom are very excited for tomorrow.

Her reply is quick.

> Really? I'm so excited I might not be able to sleep tonight.

> It'll be good to finally meet face to face. Can't wait to get a hug from my big sister.

It'll be so good to see you. You sure your mom is okay with all of this?

Yes, she was crying tears of joy. I promise this is going to work out. See you tomorrow!

After dinner with my parents, I head back to my condo in River North before I, too, struggle to fall asleep.

I can't believe I'll get to meet my sister tomorrow. Finding her has been something I've wanted to do since my dad told me the initial story of his college girlfriend and there being a possibility she was pregnant before she ghosted him.

Chapter 12

Niko

I didn't start by purposely eavesdropping on Mariah telling my older brother everything that's been going on with her new-found family. I knew that she'd begun reaching out, but I didn't realize she was planning to meet with her brother.

But then I thought, why would I know that? She doesn't know that I'd do literally anything for her. She doesn't realize my affection and protective instincts towards her extend beyond our agreement at Rapture.

When I heard her requesting a guard to accompany her to the meeting, I've never moved so fast to volunteer. My feet moved faster than my brain. I would die before I'd ever let her face something so important to her alone. I need to make sure that if something goes badly, she has me there to help.

I was glad that Misha agreed to me going with her—it allowed me to skip out on having to secretly follow her. She'd hate it if I did that since I'd be breaking the boundaries we've previously set, but my feelings for her wouldn't stop me from making sure she's safe.

This morning, I went for a run with Rasputin through Maggie Daley Park. He loves to run year-round and would run for hours if I let him. Needing to get ready to go pickup Mariah, I jump into the shower, and afterward I find a freshly dry-cleaned suit to put on; one that allows me to hide my weapons. I don't need to cause a scene in a classy place like The Langham.

After strapping two guns to the holster I'm wearing, I throw on my suit jacket. I can't leave before giving Raspy a few pets behind his ears. "Be good a boy. I'll be back later, okay?" He barks his answer, letting me know that he'll handle things here.

As I ride the elevator down to the parking garage, I hit the button on my phone for the remote start. My phone goes off in my pocket, and I quickly check it before I start my drive.

> Mariah: You'll be here in twenty minutes, right?

I smile but also feel for her. She's always on time or early. She must be really nervous if she's texting me to make sure I'm going to be prompt.

> I'm getting in the car now. I'll be there. Promise.

> Mariah: Okay. Thanks, Niko.

I spent nearly my whole life setting up to continue my path of short-term relationships. However, if there's one woman I'd put everything on the line for. I know you're probably tired of hearing me say it, but it bears repeating. Mariah Perez brings me to my knees.

Once I pull up to her building, I don't even have to text her. She immediately walks out from her building and knocks on the passenger door window for me to unlock it.

Mariah greets me as soon as she's buckled in her seat. "Thank you for coming with me. You didn't have to."

"I'm more than happy to come with you."

She's quiet during the entire drive over to the hotel. I pull up to the valet, then let them park the SUV. We're ten minutes early. I planned for this to give her some sense of control while meeting new people.

After taking the elevator up to the restaurant, Mariah tells the host our reservation is under Juan. The young guy promptly brings us back and tells us we're the first to arrive. The table that her brother reserved is slightly secluded from the rest of the restaurant, which makes me feel more comfortable. I sit with my back to the wall and have Mariah to my left.

The restaurant here is beautiful. I've been here a few times to eat brunch with my mom over the years for her birthday. She says it's one of her favorite places in the city.

Looking to Mariah, I watch her as she tries to distract herself by looking out the window. It's clear that she's worried. Knowing her like

I do, I'm sure she's having doubts about whether she'll be enough for her family.

Her abandonment wounds run deep, thanks to her mom. She deserves this more than anyone. To Mariah, family means the world because she knows how hard it is when you feel totally and completely alone. I know she's hoping that this is her second chance at having a parent in her life.

We hear the hostess telling guests that their table is right over there, and ours is the only one over here. They walk around the corner and when I see who it is, I jump out of my seat and pull out my gun. The two men who've approached the table do the same.

"Mariah, get behind me. Alvarez, what the fuck are you doing here?"

Mariah's got a look of panic and confusion over the scene currently playing out. She peeks around from behind my back to get a better look at the men who are holding their weapons on us. There's a woman with them, off to the side, being protected as well.

"Juan? Is that you?" Everyone looks stunned. I know who these men are. I'm looking at Felipe Alvarez and his son, Juan. They run one of the largest and most powerful cartels in the Western Hemisphere.

This is the Juan she was referring to this whole time? Holy fuck, she's an Alvarez. Mariah is a cartel princess.

The woman must be Felipe's wife, Camila. She's been with him for almost twenty-five years. Their relationship is rumored to be a love match and he's never strayed from her.

"I'm going to put my weapon away and then we'll talk about what the hell is going on. Got it, Alvarez?"

Both men nod and I holster my weapon. They quickly follow my lead as I say to them, "It's good to see you both."

But Felipe is distracted. He's staring at Mariah. "Mija?" He walks over to her and he's got tears in his eyes. He pulls her in for a hug, and it has Mariah shedding her own tears.

Juan steps up to them both and holds his arms open for his half sister. She immediately moves from her father to her brother for an embrace. I see Camila wiping away her own tears.

Mariah formally introduces herself. "It's nice to meet you all. I'm Mariah."

Felipe takes it from there. "I'm Felipe Alvarez. This is my wife, Camila." He motions for his wife to move closer to the table. "And I know you've been speaking to my son, Juan."

Interrupting, I suggest everyone sit at the table to continue the conversations, but I have a question of my own. "Did you know who Mariah was connected to?"

Felipe looks at me. "No. I only found out about Mariah last night."

Juan speaks up to follow up on what his father admitted. "He's right. I only told them yesterday. And no, I didn't know who Mariah was connected to. I just did a basic background check because I didn't want to break her trust and boundaries."

That's a good answer. He clearly understands that she's not had it easy and didn't want to risk her pulling away.

"Mikhail is married to Mariah's best friend, Sierra."

I see the looks of shock on Felipe's and Juan's faces. Based on that, I feel confident that they didn't know of her ties to another organization.

"Nikolai, I promise that I'm only here as a father who wants to get to know his daughter. A child I'd always hoped was out there, but only found out for sure existed less than twenty-four hours ago."

Camila interrupts us. "Perhaps we focus on the family meeting and less about business connections for now?"

Looking at Mariah, Felipe says, "I promise you that if I'd known for sure that you were out there, nothing would've stopped me from finding you. I looked for Sylvia a lot in the weeks after she initially disappeared and stopped returning my calls. We'd only been together about six weeks in total. We had an incident with failed birth control, and about two weeks later she stopped answering the phone.

"It was the midnineties, so there wasn't a find your girlfriend app just yet. I promise that I did look for her. I was afraid she was pregnant and avoiding me. But I never found her. I always wondered if maybe I had a son or daughter out there. I regret that I didn't search harder, or continue even when I didn't initially find her. I'd have done anything to be in your life when you were younger. I hope that you'll be interested in developing a relationship with us."

I put my hand on Mariah's thigh, trying to remind her that I'm here for her. Felipe notices, but smartly doesn't say anything. Mariah hasn't even said if she feels completely at ease yet with the latest developments.

Mariah begins to address the group. "I'm not sure if Juan's told you about my childhood, but it wasn't great. My mother was verbally, emotionally, and physically abusive. I know she suffered with alcoholism and likely other substances. The men she'd bring around never made me feel safe. I can remember barricading the door to my room with my big wooden dresser so they wouldn't be able to come in after my mom passed out drunk in the living room."

I give her encouragement to continue by gently squeezing her thigh, and she brings her hand to rest on mine. "One day, she'd decided that I was trying to steal yet another boyfriend. I took a beating for it, but had a big test the next day at school, so I went to class and when I came home I went to do homework and try to avoid her for a while. But after I finished, I went to see if she was home. That's when I discovered everything of hers was gone and she'd left a note telling me she was leaving and to not tell anyone."

Camila is visibly shaking from hearing how Mariah's mom treated her growing up.

Strongly continuing, Mariah tells her story. "But luckily for me, my best friend, Sierra, had amazing parents. I called her mom, Sarah, for help. Sarah and Mason, Sierra's dad, called the cops and became my emergency guardians. After a few months of going to court, they were granted permanent guardianship of me. It was the first time I felt a parent's love. They saved me from foster care and made me their second daughter. Sierra and I are still really close today."

That's more in-depth information than I'd previously gotten about the day and events that led up to Mariah moving in with Sierra's family while she was in high school. It makes me admire her that much more. She's so fucking resilient.

"Are they still living near Chicago? We'd love to meet them," Camila says.

"No, sadly they passed away. During mine and Sierra's junior year in college, they were killed in a drunk driving accident on New Year's

Eve. The five years I spent with them were the best of my childhood and early adulthood. I'll always miss them, though."

"That's so tragic. I'm very sorry to hear that." Camila sympathizes as she wipes away a few stray tears.

Felipe looks serious, but is emitting an energy of fatherly love as he says, "Mariah, I will do anything and everything to keep you safe. From the moment I learned you were mine, I loved you. I know you will take time to grow those feelings, but, mija, you are loved."

Mariah's tearing up again. I hand her my napkin since hers has some makeup on it from her earlier tears. She quietly replies to her dad. "Thank you, Felipe. That means a lot to me."

She's doing so well. I'm really proud of her for being so open. I know that it doesn't come naturally or easily for her. I'm hoping that means she's interested in continuing relationships with her family.

CHAPTER 13

MARIAH

I can't believe I'm sitting at a table with my father, brother, and
stepmother. The brunch got off to an unexpected start when
Niko and my family pulled weapons on each other. I was frozen in fear
when Niko hauled me behind him, covering me with his body until I
recognized Juan's voice. I stepped out from behind Niko's protective
stance and saw a pair of eyes that look like my own staring back at me.
My father really came to meet me.

While I tried to be forthcoming in explaining more about my childhood and to listen while everyone talked, I find myself retreating a little
bit now. My mind continues to remind me about the menacing phone
calls and angry notes the past couple months. Could they know my
family? Could whoever is contacting me be trying to hurt them?

I feel Niko's hand on my thigh. He's been such a help today. I'm
grateful he insisted that he be the one to come with me. A regular
guard may have escalated the initial skirmish and a regular guard for

sure wouldn't be providing me comfort when I'm anxious and feeling overwhelmed.

"We should order lunch the next time the waiter comes by; I'm starving after my run this morning," Niko says to bring everyone back to a more light-hearted mood after my father and I both said some pretty emotional things. Good things, but definitely heavy. I've never felt a paternal love like he's describing before. I want to believe in him and Juan so badly, but I really don't want to get hurt. When my mom left me, I put walls up. I know that I did. My therapist pointed it out pretty early on. I've done work to try and let people in. Example A is sitting next to me in all his Russian glory.

Late last year, my therapist pointed something out to me that really changed my perspective and outlook regarding my lack of trust in people and my fears of abandonment. She said, "While trauma in childhood can affect who we are as adults, being an adult now means that you can choose. You can choose to break cycles and choose to allow vulnerability into your life, because without it, you might miss out on the best moments life has to offer." I know she didn't mean it to say like the choice was an easy or obvious one. She meant that my mother's choices shouldn't continue to hold me back as an adult. As a child there was really nothing I could control, but now it's up to me.

After we all order lunch, we start to talk about more relaxed topics. I hear about Juan and Bianca growing up. I tell stories of Sierra and me when we were younger. Camila shares funny memories of her and Juan while they were dating. Getting to know them today has been incredibly special. It's something I always dreamed about when I was a little girl. I would lie awake at night wishing my dad would come save me from my mom.

That little girl is still with me, and she's feeling overwhelmed, but incredibly happy today. They seem like really nice people and Juan is exactly who he's been when we've been texting and having our weekly phone calls.

Niko and Camila both order coffee after we all finish eating. There's something that has been bothering me since the very beginning of this meeting when weapons were drawn and a brief stand-off occurred. I look at the table and speak to no one in particular. "How do you know who Niko is?"

Nobody immediately looks like they'll answer me, so I make my case. "Please, tell me the truth. I've been lied to my entire life about who I am and where I come from. I just want to know how you know each other."

That has my dad looking solemn, but I can tell he's determined to follow through on being a father to me, even if I'm almost twenty-nine.

"Mija, I'm the Jefe of the Alvarez Cartel. Me and my younger brother Jorge have been the main distributors of cocaine and cannabis in North America since our father was Jefe in the nineties."

Juan jumps in where our dad leaves off. "I'll eventually take over for Papa. I'm his heir."

Holy shit. A cartel? That's how they know each other? That's why Niko went for his weapon right away when my family first walked around the corner.

"Do you hurt innocent people? Do you treat them as if they don't matter if they get in your way?"

My dad responds without hesitation. "No. Never. We never hurt people who aren't in our world. We never participate in human trafficking, either. I swear to you, we don't hurt innocent lives."

Niko pipes up for the first time in a while after letting me take the lead most of brunch. "The Alvarez family has worked with us in the past. They've joined us on rescue missions to save those taken by Sergei Kuznetsov when he's tried to bring them through the docks. While we're not necessarily allies, we are friendly."

That makes me feel better about my newly discovered links to organized crime, but I think back to the threats I've been getting. Are they related? Is someone trying to keep me from my family because they're a cartel? Is someone in their family trying to keep me away? Questions are rapidly firing in my brain and I'm feeling dazed.

Luckily, I'm pulled out of my thoughts by Camila. "Would you maybe want to meet again this week, just the two of us? We can try that Pilates class that you mentioned earlier."

Her question makes me smile. Juan did say she was the best mom, and it's clear he might be the only one in the world not exaggerating with that statement. She's really made me feel at ease during this meal and is making an effort to build a relationship with me outside of my father or brother. "I'd really like that, Camila. I'll text you and we can figure out a class that fits our schedules."

I wonder if Camila and I will get closer over time. I hope so, and it'd be nice to have that in my life again. I never had it with my own mother, but Sarah was the first woman who made me feel like I mattered. Losing her and Mason was one of the worst things I've ever had to go through. I've avoided any situation that could replicate that pain for nearly a decade, but seeing how Anastasia and Camila are with their children leaves me longing for closer relationships.

My father stands after insisting he pay the bill, despite Niko's protests. "Mariah, would you allow me another hug, if you feel comfortable?"

I jump out of my seat and walk into his open arms. When he holds me close, I take in the smell of cigars on his jacket. I've finally met him, the man I've wished for and longed for my whole life. His words today healed some of the hurt I had growing up. Knowing that he would've been there for me if he'd known about me meant a lot to hear. I believe he's sincere about that. His eyes showed a real hurt and remorse for something that wasn't his fault. Fault lies solely at the feet of my mother.

After a minute, he lets me go and I smile up at him. "I'm so glad we've finally met. Thank you for coming."

"Of course, mija. There's nowhere else I'd rather be. I can't wait to continue getting to know each other better."

"I'd love that." I really would. I know that I want to keep spending time with all three of them. I'm really glad Camila seems open to getting to know me one-on-one outside of the guys. Juan's always talked so highly of his mom and our dad, so I shouldn't be surprised that they were as welcoming as he said they'd be.

Juan steps up to where I'm standing to give me another hug. I welcome the affection and appreciate that they all seem as openly loving as the Fedorovs. Camila rounds out the goodbyes with a hug of her own.

My dad looks at me. "We'd love to have you over to our house before Christmas, if you'd be interested?"

He wants to include me in their holiday plans? That's unexpected, but also makes my heart happy.

"I'd love to. Thank you for inviting me." We go around with one more hug for each of them, the final step in a classic Midwest goodbye, before Niko puts his hand on my lower back, leading me out of the hotel. We wait for the valet to bring the car back and he pulls me in for a hug of our own.

"You doing okay? That had to be a lot. Especially finding out that they're the Alvarez Cartel." He whispers so nobody overhears my new lineage.

"It was really emotionally draining. Not in a bad way or anything, but I'm ready for a nap or something. It was weird to see his eyes. They look like mine; I've never had that before. My mom and I didn't look anything alike. I can see Juan's smile even kind of looks like my own. All of them were really nice."

"They're good people. We've had skirmishes over the years, but they've always been happy to help with rescues from trafficking. We also don't deal in the same types of businesses, so we typically don't have too much to fight over." Niko explains more just as the car pulls up. He discretely hands the porter a twenty-dollar bill. I've noticed that him and all the Fedorovs are big tippers.

After Niko opens the door for me, I buckle up and wait for him to join me in the car. He puts his hand comfortably on my thigh while he drives me back to my condo. We pull up out front, and he parks in one of the open spots.

"We're still meeting on Tuesday?" I ask him.

He nods and says, "I'll walk you up, okay?"

Replying with a nod of my own, I let him help me out of the car and we head up in the elevator.

As he follows me to my door, I pull out my keys to unlock it, but the door is already unlocked. I look back at Niko, who immediately moves me behind him. His gun is already in his hand as he walks into my home. I slowly follow him inside, and I gasp at what I'm seeing. My condo has been destroyed.

Niko holds his gun up, ready to use it in case the intruder is still here. I look at my living room and kitchen. It's all been ruined. My books are ripped, plates are smashed, and a bat was taken to my TV. I'm sobbing at all of my things being shattered, covering the floor. This is my safe space and someone desecrated it.

Niko comes back into the living room. "The rest of the apartment looks untouched, but you should still walk through and check to see if anything is missing."

"Okay, yeah, I can look through it." I go to get a broom, but Niko grabs my arm.

"I'll have someone sent here to do clean up. Don't worry about it, okay? Do you know who could've done this?"

I shake my head, but walk into my office and open the drawer where I've been keeping the notes I've gotten in the last week or two. My hands shake as I pass them to him.

"What are these?" He reads them, and his face shows anger before he's done with them. "Mariah, how long has this been happening?"

I look down at the floor. I've tried to pretend this isn't serious, or that if I ignored it maybe it'd all go away. That's obviously not happening, especially now that Niko knows.

126

"Well, I got the first one Tuesday night when we met at Rapture, but the phone calls and voicemails started maybe two months ago."

"Phone calls?"

"Yeah, I've been getting phone calls from different numbers and there's usually a man's voice saying something along the lines of telling me to stay away, but it's never the same man or the exact same phrase. I've been blocking the numbers."

"We'll talk later about why you wouldn't have come to me with this, or at the very least gone to Misha. But what you're going to do right now is go to your room and pack a bag with enough stuff for a few days. I'm going to have someone come guard the apartment in the meantime."

All I can do is nod. I'm grateful that he's taking charge of the situation. Not because I'm somehow not capable, but at this point I'm just too emotionally wrecked to try and figure this out. I have been carrying the weight of this mysterious, and now dangerous, person for months. Combined with meeting my family earlier, I genuinely can't fathom having to make any decisions on my own right now.

I go to my closet and grab a suitcase. I start filling it with my clothes. Niko said to pack enough for a few days, so I'll just follow instructions. It's all I can do right now. I run into the bathroom to gather some of my toiletries before I put my makeup bag in the waiting suitcase. Zipping it up, I wheel it out to the main living space where I'm greeted with the mess left behind by whoever is after me. Putting on a slightly braver face this time, I don't cry but instead keep pushing forward.

"I'm packed, but I still need to grab my work bag and laptop so I can work tomorrow," I say as I pass Niko, who's still on the phone making arrangements.

Quickly grabbing all the things I'll need for work tomorrow, I pack up my tote bag. Wrapping the charging cord around itself, I also grab the letters and put them in the bag too. Not sure where we're going right now, but there's no doubt that Niko's going to tell the rest of his family what's going on.

When I have all of my stuff ready to go, I hear Niko hanging up the phone. He takes the tote bag from my hands and sets it on my table—well, what's left of my table. He wipes the remnants of my tears from my cheeks and gives me a gentle kiss on the forehead. We've been doing quite a bit of affection outside the club today, but that's something to think about later because my mind is already overflowing with anxiety. I'm not sure if my brain will ever be able to shut down again.

CHAPTER 14

NIKO

Walking into Mariah's apartment to find it vandalized was infuriating enough, but what's pushed me over the edge this afternoon is finding out that she's basically got a full-blown stalker—one that she's kept a secret from everyone. Thinking about her being scared and feeling alone is forcing me to clench my jaw so I don't yell at her out of fear. I'm scared she's in real danger and she'll try to keep me from helping her.

As she handed me the notes that she's kept, I read through them and noticed that they're not just cryptic. It's that the handwriting doesn't even match from note to note. She mentioned that there have also been phone calls going back as far as early as this fall. How has nobody noticed this happening? I know that she didn't want anyone to find out, but we should've noticed something was wrong. I'm pissed off that not only me, but my entire family didn't see it either.

I'm also pissed that she didn't feel like she could come to me, or mention it at all to me. I know that I told her this was only going to be physical and within the confines of Rapture, but I think that after the last few days where I've been touching her outside of the club, we can throw that idea out the window. I regret insisting that we sign a contract. I did it so she'd feel comfortable and I could ensure that I'd be the one she experimented with, but now the contract is biting me in the ass.

I want to be the one she comes to with her problems. I want to be the one she can rely on.

Trying to come up with a plan on the spot, I tell her to go to her room and pack a bag, because at the very least she'll be staying at my place until further notice. I'm done letting her pull away and using the contract as an excuse to stay at arm's length. I know she's feeling similar emotions towards our dynamic. It's clear that we're both bad at hiding how we feel towards each other.

I pull out my phone, and call my older brother, who answers on the second ring.

"Hey, Niko. What's up?"

"Misha, it's an emergency. Mariah is in trouble. We'll be coming to your house as soon as she can get a bag together."

"Is she okay?" I hear his voice rising when he hears that Mariah's in danger.

"For now. Can you also send a couple reliable soldiers to her apartment where they can stay inside to keep an eye on everything? We'll also need a cleaning crew to come through here. I'll explain more when we get there."

"You need us to come to you?" I know he's not just referring to himself, but our brothers and cousins.

"No, but if you can make sure they're all at your place before we get there?"

"Of course. How long?"

"An hour, tops."

"See you soon. Be careful, Niko."

"I will." As I hang up, Mariah comes back into the living room area. Tears are falling on her cheeks.

Grabbing her bags, I set them on the dented table that's now wobbly. I gently use my thumbs to wipe away her tears and give her a kiss on her forehead.

"It'll be okay. I'll make sure you are okay. I promise." That gets me a brief, shy smile. "We're going to Misha's. Do you have the notes?"

She reaches into her work bag and hands them to me. I slide them into my pocket. After she zips her work bag back up, I grab her things as she puts her purse around her neck. We walk back out to my car and I put her bags in my trunk. As I'm shutting it, a car parks behind me. Getting out of the car are two soldiers I've worked with a few times. They approach me to say hello and shake my hand.

I hand them Mariah's keys and tell them her apartment number. "Don't forget to take pictures before you start to clean it up. If you need to replace anything, let me know and I'll be sure to have whatever it is sent over. If anyone comes by, let me know immediately."

"Yes, sir," they respond in unison.

After joining Mariah in the car, I start the drive towards my brother's house.

"Niko, do you think that this is because of my new family?"

"It's possible, but this doesn't fit the MO of the Alvarez Cartel. I don't think Felipe would go for anything like that."

She stays quiet as she looks out the window as we pass street after street lit up for the holidays. As I pull up to the driveway, Ilya opens the gate. I drive straight through to the back where my brother has made sure to have plenty of parking since so many people work here during the day.

Leaving her bags in my car, I go to her door and open it. I walk with Mariah into the house and we find Irina waiting in the foyer. She runs to Mariah and pulls her in for a tight embrace. As she lets Mariah go, she says to us both, "Everyone's in the family room waiting for you two."

I hold out my hand and Mariah joins her hand with mine. It feels like for the first time since we walked into her apartment, I can take a deep breath. As we enter the family room, I see Misha and Toly right away. Vlad and Dima are here too.

I realize there are four sets of eyes staring at where mine and Mariah's hands are intertwined. I don't offer any explanation, but I do reach for the notes in my pocket and hand them to her.

I point to an empty side of the couch and lead her over so she can sit next to me.

Misha dives right in once we get situated. "What happened?"

Mariah looks to me before I give her an encouraging nod, letting her know she should share everything.

"Well, I started to get these weird random calls a couple of months ago. All of them were from different numbers and different voices. Then last week I came home to find a note taped to my door. Earlier this week there was a second note. All of them are cryptic and use slightly different phrasing, but all center around telling me to stop and nothing good will come from talking to them. There's no indication as to who the 'them' is or what I should stop. I always hang up and block the calls."

As she takes a deep breath, I put my hand on her thigh to hopefully give her some energy to keep going.

"When I realized that they could get up to my apartment, I thought about coming to you, but I didn't want to make Sierra worry since she's pregnant. I was and still am scared. I was saving them for if I did ever feel like I couldn't keep letting it continue."

She looks down at her lap, and I can tell she's embarrassed that she didn't think it would escalate further than the calls or notes.

"I really did consider coming to you, but every time, I just kept rationalizing that it wasn't serious. Then today, on the way home from meeting with my family, Niko walked me up to my apartment and we found it vandalized. Someone broke in and ruined my apartment. They damaged my furniture, dishes, books—all of it. They made my couch look like a tiger got loose. I'm just glad Niko was with me."

The last part has me putting my arm around her while she lets a few tears go. She's shaking after her explanation of the threats against her. Vlad raises his eyebrow at the comfort I'm giving Mariah, but I ignore my older cousin.

I finally speak up now that she's done talking. "We need to protect Mariah. The stalking, calls, and notes are alarming, but the escalation today is putting her at risk. This person is after her for some reason, and they're growing bolder."

Toly makes an off-hand comment. "Too bad she isn't one of us, because then nobody would dare mess with her."

"Holy fuck. You're right," I say to the room, and they all go quiet.

Dima asks, "What do you mean?"

"Protecting Mariah. The answer is to make her one of us. To marry her into the family."

Next to me, Mariah gasps and says, "No. Niko, I never want to have kids or get married. I don't want anyone to feel obligated, or like I'm a burden."

Misha looks at her with sympathy and says, "I understand how you feel, but a marriage will protect you in ways that just giving you bodyguards wouldn't. People fear our name. They know that we'll put down any threat to our family and that attempting to go against us results in total elimination."

I look down at her. "Mariah, especially after today, you'll need additional protection. You don't know which family this threat could be coming from."

The men in my family look at me with confusion, and it means Mariah has another piece of information to share to give the room a better picture of what's happened today.

"As you all know, I met my father and brother today. I've been speaking with Juan for a couple months, and today I met him and my dad, Felipe, for lunch. Well, my dad is Felipe Alvarez and my brother Juan works with him."

Misha perks up. "Alvarez? As in—"

134

"Yeah. I pulled my gun when they walked in before we all realized that we were actually meeting each other. Felipe really had no idea that Mariah was connected to us. I believe that both he and Juan didn't know. They tried to respect Mariah's privacy as they got to know her naturally. Lunch went well and they've made plans to get together again, but that doesn't mean their enemies don't also know about Mariah."

Everyone is stunned that one of the other families in Chicago is related to Mariah. I'm still not over that shock, but I know that during lunch, Mariah's smile was bright until we got back to her place. She was so excited to meet them and some fucker had to ruin it for her.

CHAPTER 15

MARIAH

Everyone in the room is still reeling from the shock of learning who my family is. Niko really just dropped the bomb on them that my dad's a cartel leader here in Chicago.

However, all I can think about is Niko saying that the Fedorovs should make me one of them. While I refuse to ever have children and was a virgin on birth control for the sole reason of never wanting to be a mother, the thought of getting married isn't as hard of a limit for me. I just don't want someone to feel obligated to be with me or feel like someone's making a sacrifice on my behalf that they wouldn't want to make otherwise. It's just always been easier to say I've wanted neither, but I wouldn't mind having a husband...

The closest I've been romantically to a man is my current situation with Nikolai. I wonder which of them will be forced to marry me, if they're actually being serious about this strategy to help keep me safe.

The thought of getting married without ever having been in a relationship is also a weird concept, but I guess the situation I've found myself in isn't typical. I have a stalker, and there are no clues as to who it could be. Even worse, there are two families involved in my life now that have criminal ties, making the suspect pool twice as large.

I'm snapped back to the larger conversation by Misha asking Niko if he's sure.

"Sure of what?" I ask.

Niko responds, "That we'll get married." He motions his hands between himself and where I'm sitting.

"Can we talk privately?" I ask him. I have two serious questions that need to be answered.

I know that for the Fedorovs, an arranged marriage is a valid answer to my current stalker problem. I know that they're doing this to keep me safe, and that their name would do everything they explained it would. But I need to have these two questions answered before I agree to anything.

I steer Niko down the hall to the foyer and sit down on one of the steps on the large wooden staircase. He sits next to me and asks me really directly, "What's going through your head?"

"I have a couple of questions before I can say yes. First, what about our contract?"

"We'd get rid of it," he responds. "We'll be husband and wife, which means a different relationship than what we have currently. I'd still be open to continuing a sexual relationship if that's something you'd be comfortable with and want as well."

That has me smiling, because I like that he's enjoying our time together. "I'd like to continue that as well. Meeting with you this week has become a source of comfort for me, and I've really grown to look forward to the intimacy we've created. It'd be nice to keep that going."

He nods. "I'm happy to hear that. What else did you want to ask me?"

"You know that I don't want children. I always said I didn't want to get married or have children. But that's not necessarily the full truth. I really just don't want to be a mom, and I know that not having children isn't a popular choice. It would be a deal-breaker for most men, so I've always just said I wanted neither. That way I wouldn't be disappointed when a man would eventually want kids. I'm sorry Niko, but I won't be able to give you any children."

"I'd be okay with that. I wouldn't mind having children, but I like my life without them too. I enjoy being an uncle. I'd be perfectly fine without having kids of my own."

"Are you sure? I don't want you to feel forced into this. I'd hate to feel like I've become your burden or that I've become a responsibility that you don't want. Once you find whoever is stalking me, we can get divorced."

Niko doesn't respond to my last comment, but instead asks me a question of his own. "Mariah, let me protect you. Let my family protect you. Will you marry me?"

Having him say this in private means that he recognizes my need to avoid attention. It'll be hard to let him go when they find out who's after me, but I'll do it because I know I can't keep a man like Niko.

I take a deep breath before responding. "Yes, I will marry you, Niko."

He gives me a kiss on my lips, and while it's brief, it brings heat to my core.

We both go back into the family room where Niko makes the announcement: "Mariah and I are getting married." He says it with a smile, almost like he's happy about marrying me. It makes me wonder why he's acting this way when he wouldn't even take my virginity unless I was willing to sign a contract that prevented us from having a relationship outside his club.

As soon as the words leave Niko's mouth, everyone gets up to give us their congratulations. Sierra walks in from where she was likely eavesdropping in the kitchen and asks me, "Are you for sure okay with this?"

I nod back to her. "I've been so scared, the past week in particular, but I didn't want to bother anyone with it since you're pregnant."

"That doesn't matter. Your safety will always be a priority to me, and to everyone in this family. I wouldn't survive if something happened to you. You're my sister." She hugs me as best as she can with her baby bump between us.

She asks me, "Why did Niko volunteer, and jump at the chance to marry you?"

I can feel my face get hot with embarrassment. My friend knows that I've been hiding something, because she asks me straight up, "Come on, Mariah, it's me. What's been going on?"

She leads me off to a corner of the family room for some privacy from where the rest of the family is talking.

"Well, Niko and I have been sleeping together." The look on her face is priceless. If I wanted shock and awe, that's what I get from Sierra.

"You're serious?"

"Yeah. I approached him at your gender reveal where I asked him to take my virginity. He initially said no, but then said he would if I signed a contract to become his submissive. Although, from how it's been the past week, it's turned into something more, I think? I'm not fully sure, but now we're getting married. I don't know how to handle these feelings I have for him other than to just go with the flow and make sure I don't get too attached because I can't be the wife he needs."

"Mariah, you'll be an amazing wife. Your value as a spouse isn't dependent on your ability or interest in having children. It's about being supportive, loyal, and loving. You are all three of those things and so much more."

I go on to tell her more about our arrangement and how he groveled earlier in the week after messing up during our first meeting at Rapture. I explain his protective streak, which started during lunch with my family earlier and continued when he brought me here after we found my condo the object of someone's rage.

Before Sierra can dig into questioning me further, Niko says to the entire room, "Mariah and I will need to get married tonight. She needs protection sooner rather than later."

That only gives me a few hours to get ready. I know that this isn't a real marriage, but it might be my only wedding. I was never the girl who envisioned what my wedding day would look like, but now that the moment has arrived, I'm wishing I had more time to prepare.

Before I can completely get lost in my own thoughts, Irina lets us all know that Anastasia is on her way over to the house from the large condo she and Maxim recently purchased.

We get started making plans for the wedding as Anastasia walks in. She comes straight over to me and pulls me into her arms. I've gotten a few of her hugs since Sierra married Misha, and each time I feel like a teenage girl all over again. It's almost like getting a hug from Sarah.

It makes me feel safe. As we're still hugging, she whispers in my ear, "Follow me, dorogaya."

I follow her out of the room where she then escorts me upstairs to one of the guest rooms. As I walk in, I see a dress hanging up on the closet door. It's beautiful. I look at Anastasia and words don't come out of my mouth. I'm speechless.

She explains the dress. "Irina called me earlier to tell me about my son marrying you to keep you safe. I figured there'd be little time for you to find a dress."

I walk closer to the gown, reaching out to touch it.

"You don't have to wear it, but I figured we'd be a similar size. It was my wedding dress when I married Maxim. I don't have any daughters, but I'm happy to share these special moments with my sons' wives."

I tear up, unable to convey my gratefulness to my future mother-in-law. I look back at the dress. It's a beautiful white silk gown that has off-the-shoulder sleeves and a sweetheart neckline. The lace detailing on the skirt makes it look elegant and timeless. We are a similar height and build, so it might actually be a really good fit without having to do any alterations.

"Anastasia, I'd be honored to wear your dress. Are you sure? This isn't a normal marriage, it's just to keep me safe while they find my stalker. I'd hate for you to regret letting me wear it later."

She doesn't respond to my comments about me wearing her dress, but offers me a smile. "You mean more to my son than you realize. Hopefully you'll both recognize your feelings for each other soon." She gives me another hug before suggesting I take a shower to freshen up. As Anastasia walks towards the door, she turns and says she'll be back later with the rest of the women.

I'm grateful for the time alone. This afternoon has been a whirlwind. Going from meeting my family, to my burglarized condo, to getting married—I'm surprised I haven't climbed into the bed to hide. The only things that are completely in my control are taking a deep breath and getting ready. A long shower is a good place to start.

Niko's been such a constant support throughout this entire day. He's been there for every moment and has never let me feel alone. While I'm terrified about who's after me, I fully trust Niko to keep me safe. I really hope that I don't let him down as a wife. I have zero clue on how to be a spouse, or even a girlfriend for that matter. I barely know how to be a lover.

Regardless, I do know that I need help and protection. Niko's the only one I trust with my body, so it makes sense that he's the one I'm willing to marry. He assured me he'd be okay not having children, but I'm not sure that it matters since I'll let him have a divorce so that he can eventually find someone who will give him a family.

He answered both my questions honestly earlier, and I feel at peace with the plan Misha and the rest of them came up with. Niko will do whatever he can and I know that he'll be a loyal husband. That is clear from our interactions at Rapture and the exclusivity clause included in our contract. He did say that we'll end the contract, but we both agreed to continue a sexual relationship once we're married. He's made me feel so good this week, and I hope that even without the contract, he'll keep showing me more in the bedroom.

CHAPTER 16

NIKO

As I watch my mom lead Mariah out of the family room, Sierra comes to stand next to me with her hands on her hips. "I know everything. You better not hurt her. I might be six months pregnant, but that won't slow me down too much."

Knowing that my sister-in-law is truly the only family Mariah has, I decide to loop her into how deep my feelings run. "Just so you know, I've had feelings for Mariah since I first saw her the day we went to the Art Institute with the girls in the summer."

She gives me a look that tells me to keep explaining myself, that she's not letting me off the hook just yet.

"I also haven't been interested in dating or being with anyone long term. Until her. I only entered into the contract with her because I couldn't stand the thought of anyone else having her, and I knew that I could keep her safe better than some random guy when it came to experiencing sex. The contract was meant to help me keep my feelings out of it, not that it worked."

Instead of elaborating further to Sierra, I excuse myself and I pull out my phone to text Sam.

> Getting married tonight. Can you grab one of the black suits from my place?

I really don't want to get married to the woman I've been pining after for most of this year in my outfit from lunch. Lucky for me, Sam's reply comes through almost immediately.

> Sam: I have about 75 questions regarding this marriage you're apparently entering into.

> Sam: But yeah, I can grab it. Where am I bringing it?

> Misha's. We're all here. Sooner the better, please.

> Thanks, man.

> Sam: No problem. I'll be there ASAP. I'll swing by my place too. I guess I have a wedding to attend tonight.

Sam will one hundred percent be giving me a hard time when he gets here, but as my best friend I know he'll show up. Throwing my phone back into my pocket, I look up to see all the men in my family looking in my direction. Sierra's disappeared from the room. My dad steps up to break the silence. "Son, why were you so willing to jump into this? We could've worked on a solution that didn't involve you getting married."

I take a deep breath, then start the very long-winded explanation of my feelings for Mariah. Why this isn't just a way to keep her safe. For me, this marriage is the one thing I've really wanted but never would've reached for had the situation not presented itself. After I tell them an abbreviated version of my contract with her at Rapture to help explain why I've spent so much time with her over the past week.

My dad gives me a look of sympathy. "Are you in love with her?"

"Another month with her, and I'll have completely and totally fallen in love with her. I feel this deep need to protect her, to be there for her. I think the only thing keeping me from saying yes right now is that I'm scared she'll never fully return my feelings."

I see my brothers nodding and my father giving me a smile. Misha and Dad know what it's like to be in love; they get it.

I carry on revealing my feelings to them. "The past week with her has been the best week of my life."

"Shit. You're down bad for her," my cousin Vlad jokes. I just shrug because he isn't wrong.

"Hey, boys, can I talk to Niko alone for a minute?" My dad walks towards the door. I get up and follow him down to my office.

"Son, are you sure you want to do this? I'm not trying to talk you out of it, I just want to know where your head is without the rest of them chiming in. You know we don't get divorced in this life. She'll be your wife for the rest of your life."

"Dad, when I say that she's the only woman I've ever wanted more with, I'm not exaggerating. Without a doubt, I want her. Even though this marriage is for her safety right now, I will spend the rest of my life trying to get her to be mine for real."

My dad nods and reaches into his suit jacket to pull out a small jewelry box. He's reverent as he hands it to me.

"This was your mother's engagement ring. We thought Mariah might like it. Plus, with the quick wedding turnaround, I didn't think you had time to find a jewelry store open on Sunday night."

Shit. I need a ring. I'll text Sam in a minute. But first, I open the jewelry box and smile. "Dad, thank you so much for this. She'll love it. It's perfect."

He gives me a hug, and when he lets me go, I pull out my phone because Sam's going to need to stop for a second favor tonight.

> Second favor to ask you… Can you pick up wedding bands? I don't care from where but make sure they're gold. Mariah's a size 5 and a size 9 for me.

> Sam: I was already making a stop. You saved me from calling for sizes. Figured you guys didn't have time.

> Thanks, man. See you soon.

I open the box again and look at the ring that once sat on my mom's finger. It's a stunning large pink sapphire center stone with small diamonds wrapping around the gold band. I look back up at my dad. "Have any advice?"

"To be a good husband, you have to be willing to listen. Don't stop dating your wife and never stop pursuing her."

I nod because my dad and mom's marriage has always been strong. He's speaking from experience. To this day, I know that he wines and dines my mom. He takes her on romantic trips and does things that bring her joy. Despite their arranged marriage, it ended up being a love match by the time Misha was born a year after they got married. They love all of us and made our childhoods the best they could while also leading a Bratva empire.

"I'm going to go clean myself up in one of the spare rooms. Sam should be here soon with my suit and wedding bands from wherever he can find something."

"Your mom and Irina were going to help Mariah get ready. I'm sure they'll rope Tati and Alexandra into making the ceremony beautiful."

Leaving my dad, I head upstairs and see Sierra exiting what used to be her room when she was Misha's nanny.

I ask about my future wife. "How is she doing?"

"Even though I'll deny ever saying this because she doesn't want to get her hopes up, Mariah seems happy. I can tell she's at least twenty percent excited for this, which is a huge deal. Do not fuck it up, Nikolai Fedorov."

That makes me feel on top of the world, but the talk with my dad is fresh in the back of my head. "Hey, Sierra?"

"Yeah?"

"Do you think Mariah could ever love me one day?"

I can tell my question shocks her, but, the ever-optimistic woman she is, she nods. "Mariah will be gun-shy about her feelings. If you consistently make her feel safe and protected, she will eventually trust you enough to let her feelings shine through. But you can't let her push you away. She's going to try to sacrifice herself if she thinks you're better off without her."

"Thanks for the advice. I'll hold on to her tight."

I walk down the hall to an open guest room and jump in the shower to get ready for my wedding.

Memories from the past week I've spent with Mariah as my sub have me reaching down to stroke my hardening cock. We haven't even scratched the surface of what I want to do with her, and now that we've agreed to continue her education, I get to be with her as her husband.

Those are the thoughts that have my dick rock hard in my fist. My hand works up and down my shaft, the pleasure coming fast. Whenever I think about how her tits fit perfectly in my hands or how tight her pussy is when I'm buried deep inside her, I realize how quickly I'm going to finish.

I watch my cum shoot against the tiles of the shower. While I would've rather been with Mariah when I came, I find solace in knowing that the next time we're together, I'll be her husband.

I finish up in the shower and wrap the towel around my waist. When I walk back into the bedroom, Sam is lying on the bed with his phone in his hand. He points to the small bag from a jewelry store and the suit I requested. He was nice enough to hang it in the closet.

"Thanks for getting all of this for me. I really appreciate it. Where'd you find a jeweler that was open?"

My friend sits up and laughs. "We've been friends since we were kids, Niko. I'll always be here when you need me. I'd also never miss the one guy who insisted he never would get married ending up marrying the perfect girl for him. As for the rings, one of our soldiers has a brother-in-law who owns a high-end jewelry store. He was kind enough to meet me after hours. You paid him handsomely for his customer service."

"Do you think that or are you bullshitting me? And not about the jeweler, asshole. The stuff you said first about Mariah and me."

"Yeah, I do. You fit together like pieces of a puzzle. I know that you've liked her for a while too. Whether or not you were going to give in to those feelings, I was unsure. I'm glad you're both getting a chance, even if it's coming out of unique circumstances."

We keep talking about some different work topics while I get dressed. I use the hairdryer that was under the sink to dry my shoulder-length hair. I know Mariah likes to run her hands through it, so I choose to wear it down for the ceremony. I don't do it often, so I hope she appreciates me keeping it out of my usual bun.

Giving myself a final glance in the mirror, I smile at my reflection because I'll be someone's husband soon. I open the gift bag from the jeweler and remove the rings from their boxes. Putting them both in my pocket, I turn to my friend, who's in front of the mirror now fixing the wrinkles on his suit from when he was lounging on the bed.

"You ready, bro?" He gives me an approving nod, like he's almost proud of me.

"Yeah, let's head down." I walk downstairs to find that my family has transformed the large family room into a romantic spot for a wedding. It's really beautiful. There are flowers and candles throughout the space. Chairs have been brought in to make a short aisle, the normal furniture pushed out of the room, and a small table with flowers sits at the end of the aisle as a makeshift altar.

As I'm looking at the details that have been added to create ambiance, my mom and Irina come back in carrying more flowers. Irina is carrying what looks like a bouquet for my bride, and my mom has a boutonniere with a safety pin in her hand as she approaches me.

"Nikolai, you look so handsome. Do you mind if I put this on you?"

I hold out my suit jacket so my mom can get to the spot she needs. "You'll be fine, honey. She's doing okay, she'll be ready soon."

She pats my chest once the flower is in place, then goes with Irina to bring Mariah her bouquet, leaving me alone with Sam. My brothers and cousins soon join us, and we work to set up some speakers so there's music for Mariah when she walks in. I'm grateful for something to focus on to distract me while we wait for the girls to come down.

CHAPTER 17

MARIAH

Anastasia is helping me get into her dress, and I see Sierra in the mirror tearing up as she sees the dress on me.

"Mariah, that dress is perfect for you," my friend says as she wipes away a stray tear.

"It really is, isn't it? Thank you again, Anastasia, for letting me wear it. It's so elegant and I feel beautiful. Do you think Niko will like it?"

"He'll be obsessed," Sierra says with a knowing wink.

We spent the past hour or so getting ready. Tati was running from room to room with Alexandra to find us nail polish, hair tools, and anything else we need. Sierra managed to put a full face of makeup on me, but I still look like me—nothing too dramatic.

When the last button is fastened at the base of my spine, Anastasia and Sierra go downstairs to make sure everything is ready. My future nieces walk in carrying a beautiful bouquet of flowers that Irina put together. They hand it to me before going to follow their grandmother. I'm alone for the first time since getting out of the shower. I stare into the full-length mirror to really get a good look at myself. I feel radiant.

I hear a quiet knock on the door to the guest room, and when I turn around, Maxim is leaning on the door-frame.

"That dress is stunning on you, Mariah. It looks just as gorgeous as when my Ana wore it almost forty years ago." He walks into the room farther and kisses my cheek. "I came to inquire if I could have the honor of walking you down the aisle?"

Appreciative of his gesture, I nod my response while fighting, yet again, to keep tears at bay. I know how hard my friend worked to get my makeup perfect, and I'd hate to ruin it because I'm weeping from how this entire family is making sure that this is still a special wedding, despite knowing its true purpose.

I've spent a lot of time getting to know Niko's parents, and they're both incredibly warm and kind people. I know Maxim had Misha's job while they were growing up, making him one of the most lethal men in the country, if not the world. But the side I get from him is a hands-on father and doting grandfather.

Once I get my emotions back under control, I respond verbally to his offer. "I'd really love that, Maxim. Thank you."

He opens his arm and I rope my own through the crook of his elbow as he escorts me down the stairs. Tati is waiting for us at the bottom of the large staircase. She asks me, "Are you ready, Mariah?"

"I am."

She nods to Alexandra, who opens the double doors that lead into the family room. I get my first glimpse into the transformed space. I don't know where to look, but before I get too distracted, music begins to play.

I see Niko waiting for me at the end of the makeshift aisle with a megawatt smile. He's changed into a black suit and left his hair down. He looks incredible. Everyone in the room stands as Maxim leads me towards his son.

I notice halfway down the aisle that they've been able to get a priest to perform the ceremony. I'm overwhelmed by everything they've done, and thoroughly impressed with what they've been able to do with two hours' notice. This family is making sure that I'm going to be protected, but also getting a gorgeous wedding.

The priest starts the ceremony, and Niko takes my hands in his and doesn't let go. We exchange standard vows, repeating each line after the priest. When it comes time for rings, I panic. I didn't get him one, but Niko whispers "Don't worry, sweetheart" and hands me a gold band that will fit on his ring finger. My hands shake a little bit as I slide it onto his right ring finger.

I know that Russians wear it on the other hand, just like how Misha wears his. So I follow tradition, and once it's in place, he puts my hands back in his. When it's his turn, I reach out my left hand because that's what Sierra did a couple months ago. When I look down, I see a pink sapphire ring with a similar gold band on the outside. I look up at Niko, who just winks at me.

The priest says, "You may now kiss your bride."

He wastes no time pulling me to him and bringing his lips to mine. I grab on to his suit jacket and let out a tiny moan before I can stop it from leaving my mouth. He uses that as an opportunity to separate my lips and have his tongue touch mine. It's a fairly inappropriate kiss, considering our audience includes a priest, two teenagers, and his parents, but he doesn't seem to care.

When he lets me go, he offers me his arm to walk me back down the aisle. The whole room starts clapping. He leads me to the entryway, where he gives me a hug and another kiss. This one is more PG, considering the lack of tongue.

"How are you doing? You look absolutely stunning. Seeing you walk down the aisle, I swear my heart skipped a beat."

"I'm doing okay. You look really handsome, by the way. I love your hair like this." I hesitantly reach to run my fingers through it.

"I'm surprised you were able to find a dress. It fits you like a glove. You look incredible."

I blush at his compliments. "Thanks. Uh, it's actually your mom's wedding dress. She brought it over when she and your dad heard about our marriage."

He lets out a quick laugh. "I thought it looked familiar. It's a timeless dress, and I know she kept it preserved in their closet all these years."

"Yeah, I'm really lucky she and I are a similar size. There wouldn't have been time for alterations."

He puts his hand on my cheek. "Seeing you walk in on my dad's arm was something I hadn't expected, but it meant a lot to me. I'm sure it meant a lot to him, too. He never got to walk a daughter down the aisle since I only have brothers."

I bring my hand to his arm and give him a reassuring squeeze. I see the ring in my peripheral vision. Looking back down at my hand at the rings he just placed there, he explains its significance. "The ring was originally my grandmother's. When my dad married my mom, he gave

154

it to her as an engagement ring prior to them meeting. While you went upstairs to get ready, my dad gave it to me. He thought it would work well for you."

"Wow. That's incredible. I will treasure it while I get to wear it." I don't want to pressure Niko into thinking he has to stay married to me longer than necessary. He has a look flash in his eyes, but it's gone before I can figure out what it means.

Soon, everyone comes into the foyer and Irina announces that dinner is ready. As we trickle into the large dining room, I see it's as beautifully decorated as the family room was. The table is set with some of the most delicate china I've ever seen. There are candles lit and place cards for everyone. We find our seats, and I'm shocked when I see Ilya and some of the other soldiers walk in carrying trays of food.

Niko laughs. "I guess everyone got roped into our wedding." I make a mental note to thank each of the guards I see in here after we've finished tonight. I know them being here means they were either doing overtime or came in on a day off because the rest of the house is still fully staffed with guards on duty.

We all enjoy an amazing meal cooked by Irina and Anastasia. They've put together a really delicious wedding dinner, and once the dishes are cleared, Tati and Alexandra bring out a small wedding cake.

I start to tear up for the fourth time this evening. I'm so fucking overwhelmed with gratitude and happiness. I also feel sad knowing that I'll eventually have to let Niko go. How I'll get through that is a problem for future Mariah. I'm choosing to be in the moment and experience joy on my one and only wedding day.

Niko notices the tears in my eyes and he carefully wipes them away so they don't mess with my mascara. "What's wrong?"

I just shake my head. I'm unable to find words that can accurately convey my feelings and what it means to me to have had everyone come together to make this happen. All to keep me safe, even after I hid it from them.

I've been either alone or with Sierra for most of my life, but being welcomed into the Fedorov family has been unexpected. I never thought I'd get to experience being a part of a family again after Mason and Sarah passed away. And now I'm an official Fedorov.

Even crazier? I met my dad and brother today.

Niko hands me a plate with some cake, and Toly starts to pass out flutes of champagne. Offering a toast, he says, "Congratulations to Nikolai and Mariah. To my new sister-in-law, welcome to the family. I know your marriage is unique, but may our name keep you safe. To my younger brother, embrace your new wife because she's a keeper." The room laughs and everyone clinks glasses.

After we finish dessert, I get up to try and help clean up, only to have my hand get swatted at by Irina.

"Don't you dare try to clean up on your wedding day. You'll never get another one of my chocolate croissants if I catch you trying to clear this table." She huffs and walks into the kitchen carrying a few plates. I listen because not getting another one of her treats would be a travesty.

We say our goodbyes and endless thanks. Niko leads me out to his car, where he opens the door and carefully makes sure the dress is inside the car before closing it. Ilya comes up to my window, so I roll it down. "Ilya, thank you so much for helping with dinner today. That was really kind of you, I'll never forget this."

"For you? Anytime, Mariah. I just wanted to say congratulations to you both." He waves to Niko before radioing to the guard at the gate to let us out.

The drive to his penthouse is short, and when he parks in the underground garage, we get all my bags out of the trunk. This'll be the second time I've been to his place. The first time was the days after Sierra's kidnapping. He insisted that he be the one to take care of me when my feet were cut up from escaping with Alexandra.

He was so adamant he be allowed to care for me. I tried to say that I could manage on my own, but he entertained none of it. He even helped me take a bath. That was the first time a man had seen that much skin on my body. He was respectful, but I could feel a lingering gaze.

During those couple of days where he was caring for me, my thoughts really shifted from thinking he was hot, to wondering what it'd be like to allow myself to let someone into my life as a romantic partner. It was a pipe dream because of everything that I had learned about him from Sierra, but during those days he was so different. He wasn't like I had imagined he'd be. He cooked for me, let me watch my shitty reality TV shows, and changed my bandages.

That was the first time someone helped me while I was hurt, and I remember thinking how nice it was. I'm pretty sure that was the turning point and the specific time when the seed was planted to ask him to take my virginity. If only the Mariah from July could see me now, she'd be shook. Not only am I not a virgin, but I'm now a wife.

CHAPTER 18

NIKO

After leaving the wedding, I drive us back to my place. Mariah's been quiet since we left, but she doesn't seem uncomfortable or uneasy about being alone with me.

I can't believe I've been able to manage the situation so I get to have Mariah in the exact way I've fantasized about. I'll need to work on building up her trust and confidence in me so that she stops fucking talking about when this ends and how this is temporary. It's not temporary, we're endgame.

I park the car and offer my hand as she gets out of the SUV. We're careful of my mom's dress, and she waits for me to get her bags from the trunk. We make our way to the private elevator that leads to mine and Toly's floor. The ride up is quiet, but the silence is broken once I unlock the door and Rasputin is sitting there with his tail wagging, very excited to see that I've brought a visitor.

"I know you were here before, but I'll give you a real tour once we get you out of the dress."

She immediately blushes, and I realize how it must've sounded to her. Despite me wanting to fuck my wife on our wedding night, I know that we'll work our way up to that. I want her to feel comfortable here. When she was here over the summer, she couldn't really walk, so she only saw my living room, kitchen, bedroom, and bathroom.

"I didn't mean it like that, I swear. I just meant to change into something comfortable so we can hang up my mom's dress." I lead her towards my room, with her bags still in my right hand. My left hand touches her lower back, and I love the way her skin feels under my touch.

Mariah shyly looks at me. "I'll probably need help. It took your mom awhile with the buttons."

"Happy to help my wife get undressed." I give her a wink before putting her bags in the large walk-in closet. Because I'm a glutton for punishment, I go to my dresser and pull out a pair of basketball shorts and an old t-shirt for her to wear. Before she even touches them, I know I'll be hard as a rock seeing her in my clothes.

She turns around so I have access to the back of the dress. The buttons go down to her upper tailbone. I start to undo each of them, noticing the hitch in her breath as my fingers touch her back.

"While this obviously wasn't the plan when I told you earlier to pack a bag, if you feel comfortable, I'd like you to move in here. I want to live with my wife and have you next to me every night."

"I don't want to invade your space."

"You wouldn't be. I want you here." Realizing I need to change up my tactics, I say, "It'd also make it a lot easier for the guards to keep you safe while we figure out who's harassing you."

"If you're sure? I'd feel safer being here with you. If I get in the way, please tell me and I can go stay with Misha and Sierra."

I turn her around with half of the buttons still done up on the dress. "Please listen carefully, Mariah. You're my wife. That means you're mine to protect, spoil, and care for. I want to do that. You deserve someone whose whole existence is devoted to you and your happiness. I want that someone to be me."

I can tell she doesn't fully believe me. But that's okay. I'll earn it.

I continue to help her out of the dress. She carefully steps out of it and puts on the clothes I laid out for her. I lay the dress on the bench at the foot of my California King bed. "Want a tour now?"

She nods and we walk back to the living room area. I have it set so that my couch actually faces out towards the floor-to-ceiling windows that provide an amazing lake view. She is looking out over the currently icy lake that makes it almost look like we're in a Nordic paradise, not Chicago.

The colors of my place were picked by the designer Toly and I hired, but she did a great job. The kitchen was designed to also face out towards Lake Michigan. I love to cook dinner there, especially in the summers when golden hour hits.

160

"There's a half bathroom right next to the front door." I point out the door, but I see she's still distracted by the view.

"It's really beautiful, almost peaceful. Hard to hear any of the traffic from the street all the way up here."

"Yeah, it's my own little paradise." I take her down the hallway that leads to my office and the oversized balcony.

"My office is usually where you'll find me during the day. I bounce between here and Misha's most days. I avoid the office we have in the Loop as much as possible so that Sam can maintain being the face of our legitimate businesses."

"He's your best friend?"

I laugh. "Yeah, he is."

She changes the subject back to our tour. "Is that balcony yours or your brother's?"

"This one is ours, but he has one too. It has a series of heaters that make it usable in winter, however, it's too cold out there tonight. There's also a hot tub just out of view from the sliding doors. Feel free to use it whenever you want."

"That'd be nice with a glass of wine and a book."

I get some pretty filthy thoughts of Mariah sitting naked in the hot tub with a glass of wine, waiting for me to get home. Soon enough, I'm having to adjust my cock, and when I look back up, Mariah's jaw is open.

"Sorry. I had a bit of a moment of thinking about you in the hot tub. Let's continue, shall we?"

"Yeah." She's got a smirk on her face now. I love when I see glimmers of her embracing her desires. I hope she'll start doing it more often, maybe even try coming on to me. Not that I'd let her be in control for long—that's my job, after all.

We walk back through the living room, since the other side of the penthouse has my room. *Our room.* There are also four other guest rooms with their own attached bathrooms. One of the spare rooms has two twin beds for my nieces. I love when they come hang out or have a sleepover. They, like me, love a board game. During weekends or summer break, we'll do a game night and order junk food that Irina would never let enter my brother's house.

I wonder if Mariah would participate. I mean she is now officially their aunt.

Realizing I've been quiet for a while, I ask her, "Would you like a snack? I know we ate earlier, but I noticed you didn't finish your plate."

"I was pretty nervous. Do you have anything sweet, though? I'm a cookie fiend."

"I think I might have some of my mom's oatmeal cookies left."

Mariah leaves me in the girls' guest room and heads on a mission into the kitchen to find them.

I see her reach into the container and pull out two of them. "Your mom's cookies are about the only thing I've had that rival Irina's tiramisu."

In the midst of her second cookie, her phone rings. She picks it up without looking. Maybe it's Sierra? Did we leave something at my brother's house?

I'm close enough that I can hear some of the call. There's heavy breathing on the other end and with a threatening tone, the caller says to Mariah, "You'll regret everything you've done. You'll regret picking him over me."

Mariah's face is ghostly pale, and I can see her starting to shake.

I whisper, "Put it on speaker."

She taps her screen and now the caller's voice is booming throughout the otherwise silent house. Rasputin comes over and sits next to my wife, offering his own brand of support.

"W-what are you talking about? What do you mean picking him?"

"You'll learn soon enough what it means when you pick the wrong side, you ungrateful slut."

That's it. I'm done with this bullshit. I take the phone from her. "Listen up, you piece of shit. I will find you, and since you clearly know who my family is, I will personally see to it that you're eliminated." I hang up the phone and set it on the counter.

Mariah has tears in her eyes and a tremor that has her entire body affected. I wrap my arms around her tightly, kissing the top of her head as she finds comfort in my embrace. Once she's settled a little bit, I walk towards the couch and pull her down next to me.

The large beige couch is one of the comfiest I've ever sat on, and the designer was excited when she made me go shopping that I found something I actually liked. To say I was not the easiest client when it came to actually picking items out would be an understatement.

"I hate to make you have to relive that, but now that we know what's going on, I have to ask you some more questions."

"I understand. I'm sorry I've brought all this trouble."

"It's not trouble and you're not a burden. Don't ever think that, okay?" I get a subtle nod and accept that is about as much as I'll get from her right now. "Is that the same person from any of the other calls?"

"No, I've never heard his voice before. They also haven't ever been this openly threatening."

I pull out my own phone to call Toly.

He picks up on the second ring, and I greet him without pleasantries. "Hey, can you do me a favor?"

"Didn't I just do you a favor by helping set up for your wedding three hours ago?"

"Yeah, but this is about Mariah."

"Shit. Yeah, of course. What do you need?"

"Pull the call logs from Mariah's phone. She just got another call and this one was the worst she's gotten."

"Will do. I'll let you know when I have something."

I hang up with my brother and look back down at my wife. She's still got tears in her eyes. She's got to be exhausted. Maybe I should bring her to bed?

She doesn't protest when I take her hand in mine and walk down to our bedroom. She's looking at me as I turn to face her. "Niko, please. I need you."

I'm still so off-kilter from having to listen to someone say such horrible things to her and threaten her that her request has me panicking. I want to do anything I can to help her. I can't deny her if she needs my body. "Can I touch you?"

She nods. "Please. You're the only thing that can make my mind settle."

I slowly take off my shirt and shorts from her body, leaving her in a lacy, white thong.

"Just so you know, I've never brought a woman here before. Seeing you here, in our room, it feels right. I've never shared a bed with anyone, so I'm glad I get to give you a first of my own."

A rogue tear falls from her already red eyes. "I'm honored."

"There's also a second first I'd like to give you, if you feel safe and comfortable."

"What's that?"

I remember from the contract signing that she's on the pill.

"I want to take you bare. No condom, just me and you. I want to feel my wife without any barrier between us. I've always used a condom and I'm negative. I've only been with you since before I was tested last."

"I'm careful when I take the pill. I do it at the same time every day."

"I know. I trust you." Holy fuck. I'm going to fuck my wife without a condom.

I know she doesn't want kids. That's a very clear boundary for her, one I'm happy to respect. If I can convince her to stay married once the threats against her have been neutralized, I'll consider getting a vasectomy. I want to take care of her, choose her. And helping make sure the burden of birth control doesn't fall solely on her is an easy decision.

My eyes focus on her gorgeous tits and I put my hands on them, giving them a squeeze before I pinch her nipples. Mariah's head falls back and a quiet moan of pleasure escapes.

I put my arms under her ass and lift her up. I toss her onto the bed and strip out of my suit. She's watching every move I make, and when I'm finally down to just my boxer briefs, I can see from here that her pupils are blown. She's incredibly turned on, and that alone has my cock leaking.

I yank the briefs down and slowly stroke my cock. God-damn, I'm about to have sex with my wife.

I crawl onto the bed between her open thighs and hover over her, placing kisses on her neck and chest as I lean on my left arm so I can use my other hand to play with her pussy. When I find her clit, I notice that her pretty little thong is soaked through.

"What's got you so wet, wife?"

Cheekily, she responds, "My husband's abs."

I smack her pussy and she yelps. I lean back on my haunches so I can remove the thong and it's then I see just how ready she is for me. Grabbing my dick, I line it up and thrust into her. She's still incredibly tight and it has me fighting back my orgasm, despite only just getting my dick inside her. I need her to cum before me, so I start to use my thumb and rub her clit as I'm stretching her around my cock.

The rhythm isn't punishing by any means; it's slow and tender. Her hands go to my hair and she gives a tight pull. The pain lights me on fire. My entire body is floating. I start to kiss her, feeling connected on a level I've never experienced during sex. It feels incredible.

I can feel her start to clench her pussy around my cock as she moans her way through her orgasm. I hear her say my name, which is indescribable. The last shocks of her orgasm have me succumbing to my own. I fill her pussy with my cum. I feel myself flooding her and when I pull out, I see my seed dripping from her.

I can't believe the most erotic sex of my life is me making love to my wife.

"We should clean you up, sweetheart."

Wanting to rinse off in the shower, I turn on the faucet so it can warm up. "Towels are in this cabinet, and if you need anything else until we can get your condo packed, just let me know."

We both wash the day off and get ready to go to sleep. When we climb back into bed, we're both still naked.

"You doing okay?"

She looks up from her spot on my chest. "Not really. I feel pretty stupid. I shouldn't have kept this from everyone. I thought that if I just ignored them, that they'd get bored or just give up. Seeing my home like that..." She shakes her head. "What if I'd been home? I can't believe I disregarded so many red flags. They could've hurt me."

"Yeah, they could've. Luckily, we know now. I'll do everything in my power to keep you safe and find whoever is doing this. I promise you, Mariah." I can feel her nod against my chest.

"I have had this eerie feeling the past few weeks in particular that someone was following me. Nothing overt, just a vibe I'd get when I was outside. It's why I've been staying home more and taking ride-shares versus walking. I tried to be safe about it, but it clearly didn't matter since they could not only get into my building, but my unit."

"You're really brave. Would I have liked you to come to us sooner? Yeah, but I understand you not wanting to stress out your friend or feel like you would be bothering us. But I promise you, I'd have helped you even before you came to me with your birthday request."

I know that we said we'd continue with sex and forgo the contract, but I really need to figure out a plan to get this woman to give our marriage a real shot. I'm not dumb enough to think she would've married me if there hadn't been these threats against her, but I plan on keeping her.

I feel her breathing even out while she's cuddled on my chest. Her leg is wrapped around mine, her arm draped across my torso. This is what I've been dreaming of since that day at the museum. "I promise to love you no matter what, milaya." Maybe one day I won't be such a pussy, and I'll tell her I love her when she's not asleep. Until then, I'll love her from the shadows and prove to her why we're meant to be together.

CHAPTER 19

MARIAH

TWO WEEKS LATER

The first couple weeks of married life haven't been too difficult. For the first time since Sierra's parents died, I feel settled. Obviously, the threats are still there, but I feel protected. It's the same way I felt after my mom left and Sierra's parents came for me. I know I'm not alone anymore, which is a heavy burden I'm no longer carrying.

Like I said, the threats are still there. Over the last two weeks, there've been a couple more phone calls and another note left for me at my old apartment.

The threat in the note was escalated, showing more anger than before. Whoever is after me knows that I moved. The note was left for one of the guards staying at my place to find. They found it slid under the door in the morning, after they woke up.

Niko has been working with Vlad and Toly to find leads on who could be stalking me. Toly found that all the numbers are burner

169

phones that were bought all over the city by different people, making them untraceable.

Today is an exciting day though, because we're going to my dad's house. Felipe and Camila invited me over to celebrate Christmas Eve. She wanted to have us over for lunch, saying it was less pressure than celebrating a big holiday like that together so soon.

I appreciate that she's trying her best to not push me too hard, and is aware that I might feel a little awkward—like an outsider. I've been texting with Camila about it since our first meeting. I'll get to see their house for the first time, Juan always says how special it was to grow up there.

Niko was cautious, but was happy to go to lunch with me. I haven't told them I got married yet. It didn't seem like something I'd want to do over a text or phone call. Niko said that we'll just need to be careful while we're there because he won't have an army of guards available if something happens. I get it—whoever this is could be an enemy of the Alvarezes, or even someone in their organization.

Whoever is doing this still hasn't made themselves known. Each time is still a different voice and different handwriting, although the most recent note was typed. While they're still faceless, I fully trust Niko to keep me safe. And I oddly trust Felipe and Juan as well. I hope that trust isn't misplaced, but my gut says they'd protect me too.

Since we got married, Niko has made a conscious effort to integrate me into his life. He took the lead on getting everything moved out of my apartment. Whatever wasn't ruined was put into storage. He helped me move all of my books from the DIY version of a library that Sierra and I built. He came home from Misha's one day and said to follow him. We walked to his office where he showed me the shelves he'd had installed. "I thought you might like to have some space for them here," he said, referring to my books.

Niko was really sweet—he sat and helped me re-alphabetize my collection until they fit perfectly. He even made sure that there was some space for when I continue to buy more books. He also made sure my desk got moved in here. He recreated my home office on one side of the large room. I have secretly enjoyed the days when he joins me working from home, and we get to be in the same space, almost like we're coworkers.

He's also brought me flowers every few days, making the apartment have pops of color from all the different vases. He makes a really big effort to be home for dinner every night.

I'm impressed by how well Niko's taken to married life. It almost makes all of this harder somehow. I hate that it's temporary and I'll eventually have to give up my husband, but I know he deserves better. He deserves children and a wife who's not shy around strangers. I never thought I'd find myself married, but now that I'm experiencing it, I wish it could be different. That it could be real. My crush on Niko has ballooned into something that has the potential to break me if I'm not careful.

I'm sitting in our bathroom at the vanity putting on my makeup when Niko comes in and kisses my temple. Another pro in the "Being Married To Niko Fedorov" list is the casual affection he shares with me everyday. Kisses, hugs, ass slaps—they all make me feel butterflies. It's very different from our initial form of contact at the club, where it was kept quiet and restricted. It's almost like he feels that he's been set free, and plans to take full advantage of touching me whenever he wants.

"You almost ready, babe?"

"Yep. I'm good to go. I just need to put the presents I have for them in a tote."

I walk over to the large tree in the living room. I find the small presents for my family and Niko holds open a bag for me to drop them in. I'm so excited to celebrate with family that I'm related to. I've never really done this. Even when my mom was around, I was lucky if she remembered Christmas at all. That's why being invited to share the holiday with my dad, stepmom, and brother is such a big deal.

I was a little hesitant given how the initial meeting went when Niko and my dad pulled weapons on each other, but when I approached Niko about the invite, he was so supportive. He encouraged me to accept the invite and said he'd be happy to come with me. So that's where we're going, to spend lunch with my family before we head over to Misha and Sierra's for dinner with his family.

Luckily, I made some more Christmas cookies with my nieces earlier this week and thought ahead to bring our gifts for everyone over there early so we weren't lugging everything around today. It's so fun to think about being an aunt. I always thought about how fun it would be to spoil Sierra's kids, and now I can. I'll be the best aunt this city has ever seen.

Niko's phone chimes. Checking it, he says, "Ilya's downstairs in the parking garage."

Niko's one ask for going to my family's house today was that we bring Ilya as backup. That way Niko can focus more on me and his in-laws while still maintaining my safety. As the elevator descends into the parking lot, I bounce back and forth on my feet, eager to get this show on the road.

Ilya's waiting as promised in one of the Fedorov SUVs. We make our way to the address Juan sent me yesterday, and when Ilya pulls into the driveway, he greets my father's guards. We get waved through, and when Ilya parks, Niko grabs the bag of gifts while I turn to Ilya. "Thank you for driving us today, I know it's not very fun for the holiday, but it means a lot to me."

"Any time you need me, I'm here. I might not be as important as your husband, but I'd do anything to keep you safe."

I put my hand on his shoulder and give him a squeeze before joining Niko outside.

Camila opens the front door before we can even walk up the steps. When we get close enough, she pulls me into probably the best hug I've ever received. It's an all-encompassing embrace that I hope to get more of in the future. She turns her sights on Niko, giving him the same hug. I see my dad and Juan standing in the entryway, so I walk through the door and pull both of them in for hugs of their own. Niko comes over to shake their hands.

My dad looks down at my hand. "Are you married?" He looks normal, but his eyes convey a slight bit of hurt.

I nod and respond for both of us. "Yeah, we are. We got married a couple weeks ago."

Niko is then on the receiving end of a look from my dad that says he better explain himself. My husband glances at me and I nod, letting him know he can share what's been happening.

Niko addresses the two men. "Let's move somewhere a little more comfortable before we dive into this."

Camila jumps between all of them. "Great idea. Let's head into the family room. There's plenty of space on the couches."

Walking into what she called the family room, my jaw drops at the ginormous tree that's perfectly placed in the corner near a stone fireplace. The home has an overall Mediterranean feel to it. There are wooden beams spanning the room, wood floors, cozy furniture, and a mantel that has family pictures leaning against the stones. I look to see that there are four stockings hung, and one has my name on it.

Niko gives my wrist a slight tug so that I sit next to him, while my dad and Camila sit across from us. Juan finds his way to a chair that sits close by.

"Well? What gives, Fedorov?" My brother impatiently starts off the overdue explanation.

"Mariah's being stalked. She's been receiving phone calls and letters for a couple of months. After the lunch we had with you all, I walked Mariah up to her apartment and it had been ransacked. All of her furniture was destroyed. That's when she finally told me, and my family, what had been going on. I married her that night to protect her. The Fedorov name will keep her safe while we work to figure out who's coming after her."

My dad's face gives nothing away, but he stoically says, "I'm so sorry you've been going through this, mija. I hate that you've been in danger."

Juan leans forward in his seat. "I want to help find whoever is messing with my sister."

His immediate response, volunteering to help the Fedorovs, touches me deeply. My dad nods along to Juan's sentiment about helping find whoever's stalking me.

"My son is right to volunteer. We will do anything we can to help you find this person."

174

"I'll talk to Misha after Christmas and get you guys involved, as well as keep you informed on what we learn."

"I appreciate that, but my offer goes beyond that. I'm determined to help protect my daughter. I know you've married her and that does give her a level of safety, but I'm offering a complete and total alliance. I've already lost one daughter; I refuse to lose a second."

I can see the distress on my dad's face now. He's really worried about me. I've never had a parent care about my safety like this. I get up and go to him. I wrap my arms around his neck and hope that my affection conveys how much I appreciate him fighting for me.

"Understood. I'm sure Misha and the rest of my family wouldn't have any objections. Let's focus on the holiday for now and we'll talk more later," Niko assures my dad and brother.

"Yes, lunch should be ready. Our chef prepared some of our traditional foods. She makes phenomenal empanadas and tamales from scratch. You'll be obsessed with them." Camila starts to lead us all into the dining room. It reminds me of the grand table at Sierra's. Their whole house is beautifully decorated and feels lived-in. I know that's a weird way to describe it, but I feel like I can see Juan and Bianca as kids here. It's a home, not a museum.

Eating some of the most delicious food for lunch sets us up to open presents afterward, allowing us to make room for dessert. Camila wasn't lying when she said that their chef was magnificent.

Passing out the gifts I brought, I'm excited to watch them open everything. I gave my dad a photo album. Inside are copies of some of the pictures I was able to save from my childhood and some from my time living at Sierra's house growing up. He shows them to Camila and they eagerly look at each image.

"Thank you, Mariah. This means the world to me. I hate that I wasn't there for you growing up, but seeing you as a little girl brings me so much happiness."

He hands a gift to me, and I carefully open the small box to reveal a pair of ruby earrings. My dad explains, "These belonged to my mother, your abuela. These have been passed down since the early twentieth century. I thought you'd like to have something from our family."

I have a family heirloom. What is my life right now? I feel like this has to be a dream. "Thank you so much, Dad. These are so beautiful."

I watch as Camila opens the handmade candle I found at a local shop. Juan's quick to say thank you for the bottle of bourbon that Niko recommended.

I feel Niko's hand on my back, rubbing up and down my sweater. I thank them for the gifts. Juan got me a laptop bag. I complained during one of our calls a few weeks ago that I need a new one for when I occasionally have to go into the office for meetings. It's a black leather bag with gold hardware.

As we start to pack up to head to Sierra's, Camila insists that we take some leftovers with us. I don't even get a chance to respond before she's handing me two large containers full of the yummy food.

We're walking towards the front door to say our goodbyes when Niko turns to my dad and brother. "I'll be in touch with you both regarding the alliance and to set up a time to formalize it with my family."

"I'll look forward to it. Thank you for taking this to your brother. I've worked with your family before and we've seen great results. You married my daughter, which makes me more inclined to make this alliance permanent, even after we put down her stalker."

"Understood. I think we'll be able to come to an agreement."

Chapter 20

Niko

I never knew how easy it'd be to have a wife, particularly one who's as amazing as Mariah. If you would've asked me a year ago if I'd enjoy married life, I would've laughed in your face. But experiencing even just a couple of weeks of marriage solidifies my need to keep Mariah.

I'm also fully aware that I'm in love with my wife. I've never experienced this level of happiness, despite the danger Mariah's facing. Every time I look at her, I know that I'm never letting her go. She's too important, too special, too everything. My place is by her side.

We got to celebrate our first Christmas together. We celebrated with her family first, then headed over to my brother's place. It was really cool to see my family embrace Mariah as my wife, not just Sierra's best friend.

For our gifts to each other, I gave her a new chair for her desk. It's a massage chair, even has a heated seat. I also gave her a bunch of books that I got off her wish list. Many thanks to Sierra for sneakily sending that to me. Mariah got me a new set of cuff links and tickets to a play that I had told her I wanted to see. That'll be a fun date night for us.

Everyone was really excited because Sierra's officially in her third trimester and baby Kira's impending arrival had us all guessing who she'll look more like. Tati is all in that she'll be getting a mini-me.

I spoke with my brothers, cousins, and dad about Felipe's offer to enter into an alliance moving forward, but specifically to help find Mariah's stalker. All the men in my family agreed that an alliance would benefit both families. We've worked together to fight Sergei and his human trafficking ring in the past. They've always provided manpower when we needed to catch those bastards as they traveled through both our territories.

We also don't compete in what we sell. They mainly stick to cocaine and weed. We sell designer drugs like ecstasy, but our main business is weapons. This alliance would allow a cut of each our businesses to flow into each other's coffers.

In our world, a marriage between a high-ranking Bratva member and a cartel princess would traditionally come with an alliance. However, usually the woman knows she's an heiress years before the marriage takes place, not hours.

Currently sitting in the conference room at Misha's house, all the men, minus Toly, are here with me as we get ready to call my father-in-law.

My dad greets Felipe when he picks up after a few rings. They both share pleasantries and a brief catch-up, even making a joke about their children getting married. Hah, children. Mariah's twenty-eight and I'm thirty, we're hardly kids. My dad tells Felipe how special it has been to get to know Mariah and how he is happy two of his sons have each found their person.

For the next hour, we work with Felipe and Juan to hammer out the details of the alliance. We all agree to sign the document on New Year's Eve. My dad and Misha extend an invitation to celebrate New Year's Eve with the rest of our family, here at Misha and Sierra's. Going one step further, Dima suggests keeping it a surprise for Mariah. She'd love that.

I want to make my wife feel special. I want to continue to deepen our connection. I'll do whatever it takes to help her start trusting that what we have is real and it's not going anywhere. In my head, I start to plan out a date for us tonight. I pull out my phone to text the manager of the restaurant I want to go to, but as I go to find his contact, Mariah's name pops up on my screen as an incoming call.

Answering the call, I say, "Hi, babe. How's it going?"

I don't get a response. What I do get is the sound of Mariah crying.

"What's wrong? Mariah, tell me what's going on." I'm starting to get flashbacks from the summer when she called Misha crying and running away from the attempt to kidnap Alexandra. I've never felt that level of despair before, even though I barely knew her. The way my stomach dropped when I heard her panicking, hasn't left my mind since that day.

Finally able to speak, she starts to tell me. "I was walking home from Trader Joe's when someone on a bike ran into me. I was able to avoid falling at first, but they noticed I was still standing and came back around. The second time, the guy got off his bike. He p-pushed me down. I lost my footing on the curb and I rolled my ankle."

She's doing her best to tell me what happened, but between her tears and fear, I can't understand everything she's saying. It sounds like someone targeted her and attacked her.

"Where are you?" I try to keep my voice steady, but I'm losing it.

"A block from our house."

I'm a bastard. I really am, because despite my wife telling me she's been attacked and is hurt, a smile creeps in because she referred to my penthouse as our house.

"Okay, I'm going to hang up, but just for a minute, okay? Toly is at home. One second, okay? I'll call right back, I promise."

"O-okay. Thank you, Niko."

Wasting no time, I call Toly. I tell him what's going on with Mariah and where she's at.

"Don't worry, Bro. I'll go get her. I'm walking out now."

I jump up and grab my laptop. I ignore everyone in the room but Dima. "I need you to come with me. Someone attacked Mariah and she hurt her ankle. I imagine she's also got a couple cuts."

"Let me grab my bag. I'll meet you at your car."

He flies through the house to the clinic downstairs and I run out to my car. He jumps in and we're on the way to get to Mariah.

Settling in, the smug asshole asks me, "Do you love your wife? I've never seen you act like this over a woman before."

I stay quiet and slow the car to a stop at a red light. Quietly, I respond, "Yeah, I do. I'm in love with her."

He nods in understanding. He knows that I'm not messing around.

Taking advantage of it being just the two of us, I ask him, "Hey, while I've got you, can I ask a confidential favor?"

"Uh, sure?"

"Do you know a number for a good urologist?"

Lucky for me, Dima doesn't ask why, but tells me, "Yeah, I do, actually. There's a guy from my residency who is doing a fellowship at the top urology clinic in the city. I'll text you the office number."

"Thanks, Dima. I appreciate it."

When we pull into the garage, I head up to the penthouse. Rushing in, I can see that Toly's helped Mariah onto the couch. She looks drained. I can tell that this is more than just a twisted ankle—her mind is struggling right now. As soon as her eyes meet mine, I can see how red they are from her crying and my feet move on their own to her.

Dima starts to set some stuff up to clean the cuts on her hands from where she fell. He also looks at her ankle. "It's probably just a sprain. Ice it. Keep it elevated over the next few days. Let me know if it doesn't start to feel better, okay?"

Mariah just nods. She hasn't really spoken since I got here and it's freaking me out.

Toly interrupts us. "I was working to pull the camera footage from the attack. I have a clear view of the man who ran into you, Mariah.

It almost looks like the way he pushed you, he wanted you to fall into oncoming traffic."

Whoa, what the fuck? This wasn't just an attack to scare her. This was an attempt on her life. She could've died.

"I'll run facial recognition and gather intel from our informants to see if they know who this guy is."

Dima enters back into the conversation. "Try to keep your hands dry at least through tonight, but you're all set. I'm gonna get an Uber back to my place. Text me if you need anything else."

Toly says he'll head back next door so he can use his office to find Mariah's attacker.

I lift Mariah into my arms and carry her to our bedroom. I need to help her get clean after everything that happened. We carefully shower together, being delicate with her hands. I help dry her off before carrying her out of the bathroom.

I gently set her on the bed and help her get out of her clothes. I walk to her dresser and pull out one of her nightshirts. "Do you need to do anything else in the bathroom?" I know she's got a whole routine, but she's exhausted. "No, not tonight. I just want to crawl into bed."

Stripping out of my clothes down to my underwear, I climb into bed next to her. I pull her close to me and roll her over so she's looking at me. I decide now is the time. I could have lost her today if this moron had succeeded. She needs to know how I feel. I can't keep it in anymore.

"I love you. I'm in love with you, Mariah. I know you never wanted to be married, but I swear to you, I will do everything I can to continue being a good husband to you."

She starts crying again. "Oh, Niko, I love you too. So damn much, but I cannot keep you. You deserve more."

I start to freak out, but she places her hand on my chest. "I can't let you give up children for me. You'd be an amazing dad and you deserve the chance to experience that."

That's what she's upset about? She thinks I'm sacrificing something by staying with her? Yeah, I'll be setting this straight right fucking now. "On the way over here, I asked Dima for a urologist referral so I can schedule a vasectomy. I don't give a fuck about having kids. I care about keeping my wife. We already have three nieces, and I'm sure there'll be plenty more over the coming years, but I can't and won't live without you.

"I want to make this marriage real, Mariah. You're my wife and I want to have you without some looming expiration date. I want to spend the rest of my life with you. I promise to be a source of happiness and support, even after we find this piece of shit."

Now she's full-on crying, but manages to blubber out, "A-are you s-sure?"

"Yeah, I'm so fucking sure."

"Th-thank you. I never planned to get married, mainly because I didn't want kids. But having you as my husband for the past few weeks has been some of the best moments in my life. I've liked you since the summer and once I felt myself falling in love with you, I got really scared that it would end once this is all over."

"This is never ending, milaya. This is endgame. You're stuck with me."

"That's not a bad place to be, husband."

184

I kiss her and pull her close. She fits perfectly against me and I can feel her falling asleep in my arms.

I can't believe this beguiling woman loves me back. I did it. I got her to stay. Now, time to focus. I need Toly to find out who this mother-fucker is that tried to kill her today. I want her to feel completely safe, and until they're caught, she's in constant danger.

CHAPTER 21

MARIAH

I wake up feeling sore and exhausted, despite a solid night's sleep. I think about everything that Niko and I talked about last night. There are still some unanswered questions, but he loves me. Despite me coming around to the idea of being married, particularly to Niko, I'm absolutely sure that I won't be having children.

I didn't want to hold Niko back from becoming a dad, but when he said that he'd asked Dima for a recommendation for a doctor who could do a vasectomy, I was speechless. Nobody has ever made me feel so seen. He was willing to make sure that the burden of preventing a pregnancy didn't fall solely on me. It assuaged some of the guilt I had for wanting to keep him.

I love him so much, and when I heard those words leave his mouth, I can't describe how it felt. I've never felt euphoric relief like that before. It was more than I'd hoped for to hear him say that he wants to stay married, and that to him this is real. I think it might've been real for me since I said "I do."

I fell asleep cuddled into his chest, but when I finally open my eyes, I find his spot next to me empty. I notice my ankle is still throbbing, but before I can do anything about it Niko comes back into our bedroom. He holds up an ice pack wrapped in a dish towel. "For your ankle."

Gently laying it on my injury, he offers me a couple of pain pills. Hopefully these help the swelling go down. I grab the water bottle I keep on my bedside table and swallow both pills. "How are you feeling today?" He shows a deep concern for how I'm doing.

"I'm okay. Sore, but I guess that's to be expected."

"All the guys are coming over soon. They have some updates on what happened last night. If you're feeling up to it, I'd like for you to be a part of the conversation. You might have something to add if anyone has questions."

"Sure, I can try to help. Would you help me clean up a little bit? I just want to brush through my hair."

He doesn't say anything, but he goes into our bathroom. When he comes out, he's got my hair comb and a spray bottle with him. We showered last night and I brushed my hair while it was wet, but after all the tears and sleep, it needs some help. I have generous waves that are almost curly, but my hair isn't thick, so I'm able to refresh it with a spray bottle and comb.

I reach to take the items from his hands but he pulls them away. "Can I help you? Please."

I nod and carefully shift so he can slide into the bed behind me, keeping the ice pack on my ankle.

"I just spray all over, right?"

"Yeah, you want it to be wet all over, then go from the ends towards the top of my head."

He listens to my instructions. I've caught him watching me using my hair masks and oil, so he knows my hair requires some maintenance. I've put water and some leave-in conditioner in the spray bottle.

He works diligently, separating my hair into sections, and avoids pulling my hair. Soon enough, my hair is feeling better. I lift it and scrunch it just enough to get the waves back.

I move to get out of bed, but Niko stops me. "What else do you need, babe? Let me get it for you."

"Just was going to grab a fresh outfit. If you're feeling so inclined, I'll need a pair of underwear, a pair of yoga pants, sports bra, and a hoodie."

He starts making a pile of my clothes on the bed, grabbing one of his old NYU hoodies. He continues helping me get dressed, and as we're pulling my head through the sweatshirt, we hear a knock on the front door. The cavalry has arrived.

Soon enough, our living room is filled with Fedorov men. As we all start to settle on the couch, there's a buzz from security downstairs. Niko answers, letting up whoever is waiting in the lobby. I'm confused, because every single male member of the Fedorov family is here. Niko goes to open the door and in walk my dad, brother, and some of their soldiers.

I get up to go give them a hug. I limp to them and am met with my dad's arms waiting for me. "What are you guys doing here?"

My husband answers for them. "We've hammered out a formal alliance with them to help protect you, but this will be a mutually beneficial agreement even after we take care of your stalker."

Juan reaches to give me a hug as well. When we pull apart, he helps me back over to my spot on the couch. Some of the men sit at our kitchen island and others remain standing. There are a lot of men in my house, so many that it's making the large living room feel small. Niko's hand grabs mine and rests our hands on his lap.

Toly starts the meeting. "We know who attacked you yesterday. His name is Arthur Wilson. He currently lives at a halfway house in a rougher part of the city. He's been in and out of jail pretty much his entire life. He most recently did a stint at Cook County for possession. He's been out for two months. According to his parole paperwork, he works at a motel doing maintenance.

"His rap sheet is long, but none of it has been for anything violent. It's almost entirely drug related. He just clocked into an eight-hour shift and we can go pick him up now."

Who the hell is Arthur Wilson? I've never heard of him before. I turn to my brother-in-law and ask him, "Why would he target me specifically?"

Vlad answers. "We won't know for sure until we grab him."

Misha follows up on Vlad's short answer. "Mariah, don't worry. We'll keep you safe. I promise. I'm so sorry that this even happened at all."

"Thanks, Misha. I just want this to be over with." I feel Niko squeeze my hand.

My dad walks up to stand behind me on the couch. His hand lands on my shoulder as he reiterates Misha's promise. "He's right. We'll do everything we can to keep you safe, mija."

Moving back towards planning, Niko addresses all the men in the room. "Does everyone have enough weapons in case this gets messy? I highly doubt this guy is some criminal mastermind, so there's gotta be more to the story."

"We're stocked," Juan says, answering for his side of the alliance.

Nodding his head, Vlad assures his cousin that they're set.

Ilya pops into our place from the hallway and says he's called down to the security desk in the building to grab spare bulletproof vests for the men.

I'm super confused on why the security desk would have access to that. My face must give away my question because Niko quietly explains to me, "Toly and I own the building. We constructed it eight years ago. We were able to add some very specific off-blueprint rooms in the basement levels, including an armory and interrogation rooms."

Our front door opens again to two younger soldiers, about Ilya's age, carrying in additional weapons and Kevlar vests. Everyone starts getting ready, but Niko takes my hand and helps me walk to our bedroom. I sit on the bench in front of our bed.

He walks into our closet and begins to change into a black tactical outfit. Seeing him dressed in the cargo pants with combat boots is turning me on. I can feel my face blush and turn warm. I'm also very aware of what this outfit means. He'll be going out into a possibly dangerous situation.

I've known for a long time what his family does, but this is the first time I'm seeing them prepare for a mission up close. The last time, when they went to rescue Sierra, Niko left me in Irina's care. I was stuck on the couch, forced to eat pelmeni and other comfort foods. I didn't have to worry about him coming back to me. I didn't love him then.

"Please be careful, Niko. I'd rather you not find this Arthur guy than risk getting hurt."

He comes to stand between my legs, giving me a forehead kiss that he quickly brings down to my lips. I love the way he kisses me, like he'll never get enough.

"Milaya, I promise I'll come home to you. Ilya will be staying here with you, protecting you."

That's actually a relief. Ilya's become something of a little brother and friend to me, and we've joked with each other when I visit Sierra's house. His place is only a few blocks away from my old apartment, so we've even run into each other at the grocery store. Having him here with me while Niko goes to get Arthur will help keep me from getting lost in my head.

"I love you, Nikolai Fedorov."

"And I love you, Mariah Fedorov."

He helps me stand up before he brings his lips back to mine. I take a brave step and push my tongue into his mouth. He immediately groans and lets me continue the kiss. Niko pushes his hips towards me where I can feel him getting hard. We're full-on making out, but before I let him throw me on the bed, I pull away. I know he's needed with the rest of the men.

"You'll pay for that later, sweetheart."

"I'll be waiting to pay in full." I give him a wink. Slowly over the past month I've felt more confident and more comfortable with voicing my sexual desires. It helps that Niko encourages me to give into those feelings by reciprocating with his own primal urges.

As we walk back to the living room, I'm hit with a feeling of complete fulfillment. This is my home now. He's my home.

Before we rejoin everyone, he gives me a kiss goodbye in private—a move that exemplifies perfectly how much he pays attention to me and my quirks. He doesn't push me too far from my safe zone in public.

My dad and Juan come over to say goodbye. "Do you trust Ilya, Mariah? He's young," Juan says.

"I trust him completely. He's very well respected and has guarded me before."

"Okay. Please be careful anyways. I can't stand the thought of something else happening." My dad gives me another hug.

I love that he's open with his affection. My family reminds me of the Fedorovs. They love openly and deeply. It's really special to be included in, and having that from my own family now is even better.

Everyone starts to file out of the penthouse, leaving Ilya and me behind.

"Are you hungry? I could make us some food." Ilya's glancing over at my kitchen, eyeing up the cookies that Misha brought this morning from Irina as a get well soon treat.

"You can have one, but don't eat them all. Those are hard to come by. You have to get run over by an asshole first," I chirp him.

Ilya doubles over laughing. "Yeah, yeah. Funny now, wasn't funny last night. I'll make some sandwiches for us."

He moves about my kitchen while I sit in one of the chairs at the island. Gathering everything he needs, he makes what look to be pretty decent sandwiches.

"Have any chips?"

"In the cabinet above the fridge."

After setting everything up in the living room, he then walks back to help me over to the couch. Instead of joining me, he heads back to the kitchen. In the open floor-plan of our house, I can see he grabs a couple of bottles of water and a new ice pack. He also swipes a pill bottle from where Niko's vitamins sit on the counter.

He unscrews the cap and pours out two pills. "It's been a few hours since you took the first dose. Niko said to feed you and make sure you take these."

I lean forward to grab the bottle of water and pop the pills in my mouth. He helps me get set on the couch, putting a pillow under my ankle and placing the new ice pack over it.

"Want to watch something on TV?"

I know I have a few episodes of *Survivor* to catch up on, so I grab the remote and pull up my show. "Do you mind if we watch *Survivor*?"

"Not at all. I have two episodes I need to watch myself, so I don't mind re-watching a couple first."

"Cool. I didn't realize you watch it too."

"My parents are big fans and have watched it since before I was born."

"Wow, I'm not even twenty-nine yet and you have me feeling old." I laugh.

"If the shoe fits," he fires back. I throw one of the pillows at him, which he easily dodges.

We settle into watching our show and after a few hours, my phone dings. I look down to see it's a text from Niko.

Niko: Hey, babe. We're on our way back. Everyone's safe.

Niko: I'll be in the basement for a while first though. I'll see you soon.

I'll be waiting. I love you.

Love you too.

I let out a sigh of relief. Maybe there really is an end in sight from this stalking nightmare.

CHAPTER 22

NIKO

We all load up into the waiting vehicles down in the parking structure. I somehow ended up in the middle row, between Felipe and Juan. Toly's driving, with Misha sitting in the passenger seat, giving directions over the radios.

We have a forty-minute drive ahead of us, and my father-in-law plans to use every single one of them to ask me more about my wife.

"Niko, how is Mariah really doing?"

I want to answer honestly, but I also want to maintain some of her privacy. While she's been talking to them pretty much every day, I'm not sure what her comfort level is, or how much she'd want them to know.

I choose to be as honest as I can be. He's deeply concerned, as clearly demonstrated by his willingness to go into battle with us to make sure she comes out of this as unscathed as possible.

"She's rattled for sure. Despite her relatively sunny mood during the meeting, she was struggling last night. Look, I promise to take care of her. I love her."

My brothers both meet my eyes in the rearview mirror, I can tell they're happy to hear me say it.

Felipe however, nods and thanks me. "I appreciate you doing this for her. I know you weren't originally together, but it's very obvious that you do love her."

"It's been really nice getting to know my sister. I'm willing to do whatever it takes to protect her. You should do whatever is needed too," Juan says. For a younger guy, I can tell he'll make a good boss one day.

"I will. Have zero doubts that I will kill for her."

The SUVs all turn off the street into a pretty isolated and deserted motel. It's rundown, looking grimy even from the car. Some of the doors hang crooked, the banisters leading to a second floor have been kicked off, and it just looks like the advertisement on the sign for clean sheets is probably a lie.

Vlad hops out of the SUV directly behind us and walks up to Toly's window. "I'm going to go find out at the office where Arthur is at the moment. I'd rather not do this room by room."

It only takes a minute for my cousin's voice to come over the radios. "He's in the basement working on a water heater issue."

Even though this guy doesn't seem violent from his record, he's a drug addict and they can be unpredictable. He's clearly able to be motivated to hurt people, example number one being the assault on Mariah yesterday.

We unload from the SUVs, heading straight towards the basement. I keep my hand on my weapon and yell for Arthur. We enter a large, open area at the bottom of the staircase. I'm greeted with the disheveled man from the video yesterday. He looks around the room, trying to find an escape, but it's clear this basement doesn't have an easy exit from where we're all standing.

Deciding to be stupid, he tries to run. Juan bumps into me as he follows. Arthur gets maybe ten feet before Juan tackles him to the ground like he's an NFL linebacker. Vlad walks over to them, producing zip ties from one of his pockets. We help Juan get him cuffed, then we lift and carry him out to one of the SUVs. Guards climb in and sit either side of him so he's blocked in.

I get back into my own spot in the car and we make our way back home. Toly clicks an opener once he's parked in the underground garage, revealing a hidden elevator that brings us directly into a section of basement that is off the official architectural plans. Vlad opens the door to the closest interrogation room.

The room is bleak. It's got an old, rickety wooden chair with armrests sitting in the middle of the room, above a drain. There are a few lights dangling from the ceiling and a table along the far wall. Already laid out are some tools to use when we nicely ask Arthur why the fuck he's trying to hurt my wife.

Once he's been forced into the chair, Arthur starts to panic too much for my liking.

"Vlad, can you make sure he can't kick his legs?"

"Of course, Cousin. I'll fix his hands too." Vlad laughs. He's our head enforcer, so he's usually the leader during something like this. Unfortunately for Arthur, he hurt my wife. That makes this my time to shine.

Vlad's soon got Arthur's ankles zip tied to the legs of the chair and his wrists to the armrests. It's showtime.

I turn to Felipe and Juan, giving my father-in-law a nod, letting him start us off.

"Why did you target my daughter?"

We're met with silence. He's facing down myself, Vlad, Dima, Juan, and Felipe. Most people would be shitting bricks at the prospect of facing down two criminal factions. Arthur? He's seemingly more bothered we interrupted his day at work.

He's sitting there with a smug grin, so I walk to stand directly in front of him and let my fist meet his jaw. Blood starts to drip from his mouth down his chin. I continue to throw punches. By the time I let up, he's going to have a black eye along with some bruised ribs.

I'm starting to get impatient with this fucker's ability to stay quiet and protect whoever is really coming after Mariah.

Again, I ask him, "Who's stalking my wife? Why target her? How the hell do you even know who Mariah is?"

We're met with silence still. This guy has to have a death wish.

Getting pissed at the continued lack of responses, I tell my cousin, "Get me a blade. It's alright if it's a bit rusty."

I can see Arthur start to crack as Vlad hands me a knife. His throat bobs in a desperate attempt to swallow his fear. Sweat and blood now cover his shirt. We're finally getting somewhere, so I inquire again, "Why the fuck were you attacking my wife yesterday?"

He refuses to answer still, so I put my hand on his forearm to hold him steady. "Vlad, I could use some help. Hold out his pinky finger. Keep it straight."

I look at Arthur, giving him another chance, one he doesn't deserve, to answer me. Once I see that he's determined out of some weird loyalty to stay quiet, I put the blade against his pinky finger and begin to slice it off.

Immediately yelling in pain, he starts to rock back and forth in the chair. Having to raise my voice louder than his, I demand answers. "Why? Why did you think you could get away with hurting my wife?" I point to Felipe. "How could you hurt his daughter?"

I pick up the blade again and go to cut a second finger off before he finally opens his bloody mouth. "Th-there's a woman that was staying at the motel. She gave me drugs in exchange for following a girl named Mariah Perez. She offered me double if I could hurt her and keep her away from her brother and father."

I look over my shoulder at where both men are fuming. A woman is after Mariah? Why? She's literally the sweetest, kindest woman. How could she have enemies?

Giving in to the pain of his finger being cut off, Arthur decides to vomit. Luckily, it'll be easy to hose off into the drain nearby, but the smell is foul.

He's not off the hook yet, though. All he's really told us is that a woman is behind this. "Tell me more. Who is she? What does this woman look like?"

Finally feeling talkative, Arthur says, "I don't know her name. I just needed a fix, man. The woman's probably in her early fifties and is a hardcore addict. Something's not right with her." He motions his still zip-tied-hands to his head, like as if to say she's not all there mentally.

"What else?"

"She, uh, she moved out this morning when she left me some gear in exchange for hurting the girl."

Fuck. She's in the wind.

I walk towards the hallway and motion to both Alvarez men to follow me. Vlad stays in the room to keep an eye on our guest.

Addressing both of them, but mainly Felipe, I make a suggestion. "Would you be cool if we let him go? He clearly isn't her stalker and knows basically nothing. This woman is who we need to focus on. I'll have some guys dump him at a hospital and keep an eye on him in case this woman comes back. We already took his finger and he's too scared to say anything to anyone. He'd end up back in jail for hurting Mariah."

"Nikolai, I don't like it, but I understand your logic. You're her husband; this is your decision." Felipe gives Juan a pocketknife.

We all walk back into the room. Juan cuts Arthur's restraints while Dima approaches the man to render some basic first aid. He puts a bandage over the finger, telling him to go to the ER.

We load him up into one of the SUVs with three guards and instruct them to drop him at the nearest hospital and to follow him until further notice.

Looking back at everyone still down here, I notice they all look exhausted. This whole situation has had everyone on edge. "Let's all go home for a while. We can recap tomorrow. I want to go home to my wife."

We say goodbyes and I'm riding the elevator to our floor in less than three minutes. I walk in to find Mariah and Ilya watching some competition show. "Go home, Ilya. Thanks for staying with her while we took care of things."

"Of course. It's an honor to help the family. Let me know if you need me to stop by tomorrow. I'm off, but I'll be here if necessary."

"Appreciate that. Have a good night." I pat his shoulder.

"Bye, Ilya! Thank you for hanging out with me." Mariah pops her head above the back of the couch. Ilya just smiles at her and nods.

"Should I be jealous, wife?"

"Of a kid I think of as a little brother? Probably not."

I go join her on the couch, lifting her up so she's sitting across my lap. I give her a very watered-down version of what information we got from Arthur Wilson, including that we know her real stalker is a woman.

"Arthur said she's in her early fifties. He didn't give a physical description, but Toly will work on finding her based on places that she and Arthur interacted. Do you have any idea who this could be?"

She ponders for a minute, then shakes her head. "No, I really don't. I mean it could be a disgruntled former client, but this seems way to excessive for something I did at work."

"We have a lot of people on this. Let's make some dinner."

Before she can even speak, her stomach growls, effectively agreeing for her.

CHAPTER 23

MARIAH

"We should go shopping," Niko says, standing next to me as we brush our teeth.

"Why do we need to go shopping?"

"Tomorrow is New Year's Eve and my family goes all out. We get dressed up to celebrate with our organization at large. There's a lot of people that come, and I thought it'd be fun to go shopping to find you something new to wear."

I shake my head. "That's really sweet, but I don't need a new dress."

He comes to my side of the vanity to stand behind me. His hands lace around my waist, while his toothbrush sits at the side of his mouth. "Please."

Looking in the mirror, his faux-puppy dog eyes meet mine. My husband's quite the charmer. I can feel my resolve disappearing. "Fine. But nothing extravagant."

Before I can even get my wits about me, he's whisked me off to a gorgeous dress boutique near Michigan Avenue. I almost don't recognize Niko as he works with the saleswoman to select some gowns for me to try on. I overhear them talking about my skin tone, hair color, even my personal style. I had no idea he was such a secret fashionista.

Soon, I'm being led to a dressing room area, where the saleswoman, Anita, helps me get into the beautiful gowns. I walk out to a mirrored area where Niko found a spot to sit. I give him a fashion show as I make my way through trying on the dresses that they chose. He smiles and gives my ass a smack as I walk past.

I look at the next dress she has for me to try on, and I see this stunning, deep navy-blue dress. The cut shows some cleavage, but the showstopper is the bare back of the dress. I turn to face the small mirror in the fitting room. I love it. This is my dress. I just hope he likes it as much as I do.

She pulls the curtain back so I can show Niko. I see the moment his eyes shift to something darker, more feral. He stands and stalks over to me. He looks at Anita, who's obviously enjoying the interaction between the two of us.

"Anita, would you be so kind as to ring this dress up for us? Please also select a pair of shoes. She's a size seven. I'll assist my wife in getting back into her street clothes."

"Of course, Mr. Fedorov. I know just the pair." She hurries off, no doubt thrilled with her commission today.

"In the fitting room. Now," he all but growls into my ear.

I quickly listen to him, and as he closes the curtain behind us, he tells me to stay quiet. In equal parts desire and shock, I watch him drop to his knees in front of me. His hands begin to lift the skirt of my dress. He carefully brings my still slightly sore ankle around his shoulder, giving him access to what he's after—my pussy.

"Be quiet, or I stop," he says quietly as his fingers move my underwear to the side. I clench my jaw the second I feel his tongue make contact with my clit. The suction feels overwhelming. My hips start to move of their own accord, and I soon realize I'm riding his face. The feeling I've come to associate with an approaching orgasm takes over. I can barely think when I bite my finger to avoid letting out a single noise. I'd be mortified if sweet Anita heard me cum on my husband's face.

I ride out the rest of my orgasm, then Niko fixes my underwear and wipes his face on the back of his hand.

"Mariah, you're such a good girl to cum on my face like that where anyone could've heard you or walked in."

Heat rushes to my cheeks I hadn't even thought about someone accidentally walking in on us. Happy that it didn't happen, I turn to the side so he can unzip the dress since I need to change back into my clothes. His warm hand causes goosebumps to crawl up my back. I hope I never get tired of feeling his touch against my skin.

We find Anita at the counter, where she's got shoes bagged, and she takes the dress from Niko to package for us. Niko pays for everything and just winks when I thank him for today.

On the drive back home, he asks me, "How would you feel about going back to Rapture on New Year's Day? We haven't been there since before we got married."

Feeling extra confident after our encounter in the dressing room, I say, "I'd love to."

***

I walk out of our closet after getting into my dress. I look in the large floor-length mirror in our room and I feel proud of the woman I see looking back at me. My husband approaches me. Wrapping his arms around my waist, he kisses the crook of my neck.

He moves to pull something out of his pocket and produces a radiant necklace, putting it around my neck. It's a pink sapphire, matching my ring. I gently touch the center stone, looking at Niko in the mirror.

"I had it custom made to match. I thought you might like it."

"I love it. Thank you so much. It's so pretty."

"Fuck, babe, I can't wait to kiss you at midnight. Starting my year off the best way possible."

"You know that I love you without all these gifts, right? You don't have to spoil me." I've never had anyone treat me this way before, and it's hard for me to accept.

"I do need to spoil you, and I plan on doing it for the rest of my life." Leaning down, Niko kisses my cheek before tying his bow tie.

If he'd said that before he told me everything the night of my assault, I'd have thought he was kidding. I now know that he means it, though. He never plans to let me go, and I'm going to hold on just as tightly to him, but I'm still a bit insecure. I look at him, hoping for reassurance. "How can you be sure that we'll have forever? Yes, we've said we love each other, but so much can change."

After letting me voice my concerns without interruption, he puts both of his hands on my cheeks. "Baby, I promise you I'll do everything humanly possible to make sure that you live a happy, full life. You make me feel loved in ways that I've never experienced before. You do so much for me without even realizing. Your mere presence calms me. You're never getting rid of me."

I laugh, but believe him. He's not someone who just says things, he means them. I'm so grateful he stepped up like he did, and for him being so patient during our sexual interactions, barring his reaction after our first time.

"You know, I realize this will make me seem like a dick, but I can't tell you how happy it makes me that I'll get to be your first and only. I know how special it is, what you given me. I'll never betray your trust."

"Enough with those sweet words of yours. You'll make me cry, and we don't have time for me to redo my makeup."

Niko grabs his keys, and I get my purse before we make our way to the SUV. On the drive over to my friend's house, I think about everything that this past year has brought me. I planned for a quiet life, one that was adjacent to Sierra's so I could continue to be her best friend and sister. I started this year with faint goals to maybe lose my virginity, but marriage wasn't even a thought.

The list of everything I've gained this year is extensive. I've found someone I love and married them—even though we might've done that in reverse. I found and met my father, Juan, and Camila. I became an aunt to two tenacious girls with a third on the way.

Despite my dad's job choice, he seems like a good man. He's followed through on everything he's promised. He reminds me of Maxim in many ways. I'm excited to spend more time with that part of my family in the New Year. It's been fun to see just how similar Juan is to the Fedorov men—protective and viciously loyal.

Spending Christmas Eve with them was easily a highlight of the past year. However, my wedding day to Niko is, and will always be in the top spot. I'm brought back to the present when I feel Niko squeeze my thigh. I look up and realize Ilya is waving to me from the gatehouse. I wave and smile back, happy to be here with my husband.

Chapter 24

Niko

I park next to Vlad's Maserati and help my wife out of the car before we head inside. Everyone greets us as we walk in, but Misha whispers in my ear, "We'll need to talk before dinner, in my office."

I turn to look at him. "Should Mariah come with?"

He gives me a solemn nod, indicating to me that it's about her stalker.

I go to say hello to my sister-in-law. "You look radiant, Sierra." Her smile brightens as I kiss her cheek.

She sees Misha starting to gather everyone to go talk in his office, but I need to make sure that if it's not good news, Sierra's aware. "This meeting might change Mariah's mood. She might need you after."

"I'll be here for her, always."

Finding Mariah, I tell her that we're going to Misha's office for an update. We join everyone else, including Tati, in my brother's large office. I sit on the far couch with Mariah while Tati starts the meeting by sharing her computer screen on the large TV hanging on the wall.

Toly is the first to talk, though. "Tati and I worked last night on checking the surveillance cameras at the nearest street corner to the sketchy motel we picked Arthur up at to see if we could spot anyone who would fit the description of the middle-aged woman he told us about."

I feel Mariah tense and harden her posture at the blurry image of the woman they think could've hired Arthur. Mariah's got tears in her eyes as her face goes quite pale. She leans into me, looking for support, and I move my arm around her shoulder, letting her get even closer.

"Babe, do you know who that is? Have you seen her before?"

Mariah nods and tries to compose herself, but the tears continue to fall. Finally she's able to let us know who the woman is. "The woman in that picture is my mother, Sylvia Perez."

I hear someone drop an f-bomb, but I'm not sure who. I'm too focused on my wife. Apparently, so is my niece. Tati walks over to us on the couch and gives her new aunt a hug, which Mariah happily returns. I'm really proud of Tati—she's going to be a great Pakhan one day. She's grown a lot in her ability to show compassion and empathy.

Vlad asks for more information. "Is there anything that you can tell us about her? If you feel comfortable."

I reach to the coffee table and grab a few tissues, handing them to Mariah. She composes herself for a moment, but I can see the determination to see this through take hold in her facial expression.

"I haven't seen the woman in twelve years, but my mom was an alcoholic my entire childhood. As I grew older, she became more verbally and physically abusive. Everything from telling me I'm a whore to slaps across my face. There were worse situations, but when I was sixteen, she ran off with a new boyfriend, a drug addict who didn't want a kid in the picture.

"I found out she'd left because there was a note on the kitchen counter when I came home from school one day. The note said that she knew I wanted her boyfriends and she wasn't going to let me have them. I was still a child, and I certainly didn't want any of her creepy boyfriends. That didn't stop them from making suggestive comments to me or trying to touch me."

I'm fuming. She's told me a lot of this before, but hearing again everything she went through has me wanting to punch something.

She continues explaining all there is to know about Sylvia. "When she abandoned me, that's when Noah and Sarah, Sierra's parents, took me in and eventually gained guardianship of me. I haven't seen that woman since the morning of the day she left, when I was headed out the door to catch the school bus. I have no clue why she'd be sending me threats, let alone bribing a drug addict to hurt me. She's been out of my life for over a decade."

How anyone can do this to their own child, I'll never understand. The woman who gave birth to Mariah is one of the worst of kinds of people—one who hurts children.

I ask my family, "Can we get more background on Sylvia? Where's she been since she left Mariah?"

Toly nods. "Yeah, I've already got my team on it. They should hopefully have something tonight or tomorrow. In the meantime, we should rejoin the party and do our best to enjoy the evening." He looks sympathetically at my wife, who's still snuggled close to me.

Everyone files out of the office, leaving me alone with Mariah. I move my arm so I can help her up from the couch. I guide her into my own office for some additional privacy. I close the door and she immediately walks into my embrace. I walk her to the love seat I have in here and let her sit on my lap while I hold her tight, allowing her to get every emotion out that she needs to.

I rub her back and tell her how much I love her. I tell her how strong she is, that we'll put a stop to it all.

From my office, I can hear a commotion at the front door. Ah shit, her family probably just got here. Maybe this will help distract her from everything that has happened, even if just until midnight.

We'll need to give her dad and brother an update on the situation, but that can wait until after she says hello to them. I don't know how Felipe will take Sylvia being the one behind everything, but I anticipate Juan losing his shit.

"Alright, sweetheart. I have a surprise for you."

She laughs from behind her tears. "I'm not sure I can handle more surprises tonight."

"I promise that you'll love this one."

Mariah climbs off my lap and goes to check her makeup in the mirror I have hanging on the wall. She straightens her dress, and when

I kiss her forehead, she gives me the first real smile since we arrived. "Come on, babe. Let's go get your surprise."

Everyone's still in the large foyer, welcoming my in-laws to the party. Mariah leaves my side and runs to her dad, stepmom, and brother. She gives them hugs and kisses, obviously excited to see them. It makes me happy that we had the forethought to make their appearance tonight a surprise. It couldn't have happened at a better moment.

Irina whistles so loudly that she gets everyone's attention. "Dinner is ready if you all are!"

I see Felipe offer his arm to Mariah as they walk into the dining room. We all follow. The room has been decorated with New Year's balloons. The large table was removed in favor of a few smaller tables. There are maybe forty people here in total. A lot of our higher ranking men are here with their wives or girlfriends.

We all enjoy a delicious meal courtesy of Irina and my mom. They've made traditional Russian dishes, but Mariah was so happy to see that Camila had brought some homemade tamales and ajiaco, which everyone devours. Conversation flows among the tables. Camila and Felipe brought my nieces some small belated Christmas gifts, which both of the girls are grateful for.

After we finish dinner and some coffee with dessert, most of the guests leave, with only our family and the Alvarez contingent still standing. With the smaller group, we all go to the family room and start playing some board games. My family loves anything competitive, which makes board games and card games a huge part of our holidays. I'm happy to see Juan jumping right in on the fun, sitting next to Mariah, who has a genuine smile on her face.

The parents are all sitting on the couch watching the countdown on TV. I know my parents have always respected Felipe and Camila—my dad's always said that Felipe is a respectable man who believes in loyalty. A traditional leader, who demands respect not by force, but because he's earned it.

Misha gets my attention, and I know why. He goes to pull Felipe and Juan aside so we can give them news that we figured out who's after Mariah. Out in the hallway, my brother tells them that Sylvia is the one who's been doing all of this to Mariah.

Felipe is fuming. He starts to pace around the foyer. He keeps his voice low so he doesn't disturb everyone in the family room. "Why the hell is my ex-girlfriend, Mariah's own mother, doing this to our daughter? What kind of scum did that woman turn into?"

Juan's equally, and understandably, pissed off, but he focuses his energy. "Whatever you need to end this, you have it. We also want to be there when you take her down."

Felipe nods his agreement with what his son is offering. They want to keep her safe just as much as I do.

CHAPTER 25
MARIAH

When Niko and Misha led my dad and Juan out to the hall, Sierra and I joined the other ladies on the couch. We start to talk about Kira's upcoming arrival in the New Year. The last couple of months will fly by; maybe not for Sierra, but for the rest of us.

"I can't wait to get some baby snuggles from my niece!"

"You'll have to fight for time with her." Anastasia laughs. "I remember when the girls were born, all of the boys would argue over who was next to hold them."

Sierra jokes, "I'm sure they won't have grown out of that, except now they'll have Mariah and the girls to contend with."

We're all laughing. Camila tells us how Juan was just as obsessed with Bianca when she was a baby. Anastasia holds her hand, giving it a squeeze.

Sierra leans against me as she rubs her hand over her bump. "Are you happy, Mariah?"

"Yeah, I am. I really am. Getting married was the best thing for me and I know it. Niko was meant to be my husband."

All of us turn as the four men walk back in. I can tell based on my dad's and brother's faces that they know about Sylvia. Neither says anything, but Juan gives me a smile and a nod. I know it'll be okay. I have more support now than I've ever had. I feel that as Niko sits beside me. I'll be starting the New Year surrounded by so much love.

When the final countdown on the TV begins, everyone stands up. Some are holding glasses of champagne or sparkling juice, while others are standing with their significant others. Niko pulls me close to him, and with ten seconds left, he starts to kiss me. I feel his tongue come into my mouth and we share a deeper kiss. His lips are warm and soft against my own. I can hear the cheers as the clock hits midnight, but our kiss continues.

When Niko finally pulls back, he smiles and says, "I love you so much. I wanted to end the year and start the year doing my favorite activity: kissing my wife."

I throw my head back and let out a laugh. "I love you too. So much."

Everyone starts giving hugs and kisses, celebrating the start of a new year. The best wishes soon turn into goodbyes as everyone starts to leave. Toly comes up to us, asking for a ride home since he'd been drinking. The three of us head to the car, and Toly insists I sit in the passenger seat, despite my protests considering our size difference, but he hears none of it.

We make small talk about random stuff as Niko drives us home. He says he wants to try and renovate one of our spare rooms into an office for me.

"But I like sharing an office with you."

He laughs. "You do? I really don't mind building you an office."

"No, please, I want to keep sharing."

From the back seat, Toly pipes up. "Oh, isn't that precious. You are a good husband, Niko. Spoiling your wife like you should."

Niko slows to a stop at the red light and turns to the back seat to punch his older brother, who feigns injury. When the light turns green, Niko accelerates, but before he can make it through the intersection, I see a set of headlights coming towards the SUV at full speed out my window.

I feel the impact, and as the car starts to roll, I feel myself passing out. The next thing I know, Niko's trying to get my seat belt unbuckled. I can hear Toly trying to yank on the door to get it open.

"Mariah, stay with me, okay? We'll get you out of here. I promise." I can hear the panic in Niko's voice. He's worried, but trying to hide it. He and Toly carefully work to get me out of the car. Once I'm free, I can smell the leaking gasoline. While the two men carry me to the sidewalk, I see Misha and Ilya jumping out of a car that just pulled up. Either Niko or Toly must've called for help.

I'm still feeling dizzy after waking up in the car. My keep eyes trying to close, despite me attempting to stay awake. Ilya comes to sit with me and instructs me to keep my eyes open. I do my best, but I see through some hazy vision that the guys are going to check on the other driver. When they open the door, I can hear a woman screaming. My stomach drops. I know that voice. *Sylvia is here.*

Toly and Misha are trying to pull her from the car but she's fighting. It ends up taking them and another soldier to control her. She's probably high on something. The moment she sees me propped against a building on the corner, she starts to yell even louder. The men are still holding her and they take her to the opposite street corner.

With her contained, I can feel the pain starting to set in. I look down and see blood coming from my abdomen. I already knew I was bleeding from my forehead because I felt it dripping down my face. I turn to look at Ilya. "How bad is it? Am I gonna be okay? I feel really cold."

His look of concern tells me that whatever he's seeing is serious. "Just try to stay awake, okay? I'm gonna need you to put pressure on your stomach." He guides my hand over the bleeding wound and presses down. Niko re-joins us on the corner. "An ambulance is on the way, okay, sweetheart?" I nod.

I hear my mom carrying on again. She's just yelling nonsense at this point. "I should've never had you! I regret you every single day. You're an ungrateful slut!"

I know that none of what she's saying is true, but it opens wounds from childhood. I can feel tears starting to fall. I'm so ashamed that this is the woman who gave birth to me. Why couldn't I have had Sarah, Anastasia, or Camila? Those three are amazing moms.

I can finally hear sirens. Niko is comforting me. "Don't listen to her, Mariah. She's high."

Police and the ambulance finally arrive. Niko reassures me, "Don't worry. The police on scene are all on the Fedorov payroll, okay? They won't let her get away."

Two EMTs come over to where I'm sitting and they have a gurney with them. I've been trying to keep pressure on my stomach with Ilya's help, but the blood is still seeping around my fingers. The dizziness is

216

becoming stronger and I'm having to fight even harder to keep my eyes open.

One of the paramedics takes over and joins me on the sidewalk. Ilya goes to help out with my mom, who's still carrying on. I've completely tuned her out. Niko is fussing over me. I know he's worried. My injuries must look bad for him to be outwardly showing fear when he's been trained his whole life not to show emotion to the outside world.

"We're going to put you on the stretcher and take you lights and sirens to the hospital, ma'am."

The pain when they move me is intense. I think I yell out when they strap me to the gurney. I can feel it getting more difficult to breathe. Niko grabs my hand while the other EMT brings gauze to my stomach wound. The pain worsens when I get jostled during the transfer into the back of the ambulance.

I can hear Niko nearly yelling at someone, "That's my wife! I'm not leaving her alone."

As the back door closes, I feel Niko beside me. The paramedics continue to work around me, but I know that Niko's with me and that's all that matters. I know everyone keeps telling me to stay awake, but I'm so sleepy. I'll just close my eyes for a minute, but as I do Niko tries to say something to me. I can barely hear him, his voice sounds a million miles away.

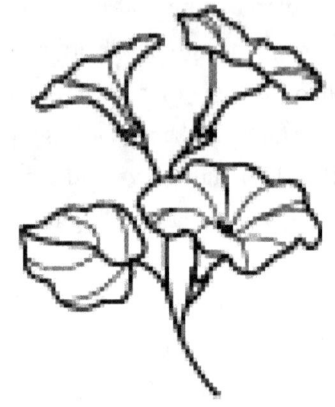

CHAPTER 26

NIKO

After fighting my way into the back of the ambulance, I try to stay calm in the jump seat they have for passengers. I want to hold Mariah's hand, but she's strapped to the gurney.

I hear the sirens turn on as we begin moving, but Mariah's eyes are closing. I see her head loll to the side as she loses consciousness again.

The moment the accident happened, I was worried about my wife. We were hit directly on her side and it sent my SUV rolling a couple of times. I was able to get out, as was Toly, but we both saw Mariah stuck hanging upside down, trapped and unconscious.

We worked to get her free. I could see blood everywhere. Her shirt was soaked with it and her forehead was also oozing. It took us a while, but we got her out, and luckily Misha had arrived, since we were only a couple minutes from his house. He had brought Ilya and a couple of soldiers with him for backup.

Ilya went straight to be with Mariah, which I was grateful for. I know they've gotten close, and Mariah sees him as a kid brother. It's kind of funny considering I've seen Ilya kill people. Nonetheless, he kept her calm and conscious while we waited for the police and ambulance to arrive.

When my brothers pulled the other driver out of the car, I almost couldn't believe my eyes. Being dragged from the small four-door sedan was Sylvia. She purposely ran a red light to hit my car. This was deliberate. She was aiming to kill her daughter.

From beside me, I hear the paramedic shout to the driver of the ambulance, "Drive faster! She's going downhill!"

Things start beeping and the EMT tells me, "She's losing too much blood, it's causing her blood pressure to tank." The man tries to slow the bleeding as best he can while in a moving vehicle.

"I can see a large piece of glass stuck in her abdomen near her lower ribs. Part of it must've broken off because I didn't see it until I cut her shirt open."

"What can you do?" I resort to pleading. "Please, you have to help her. I can't lose my wife."

"I'll do the best I can, but she's struggling to breathe."

I can see her chest moving up and down, but it's the opposite of her breathing. I can see the EMT start to show some panic. "She might have a collapsed lung."

He puts an oxygen mask over her mouth and asks his partner, "How much longer?"

I feel some of the tension I'm carrying leave my body when I hear the driver respond with, "We're two minutes out!"

This ambulance is going to need to be hosed down after they get me and Mariah to the hospital. She's really struggling, and I hate that there's not a single thing I can do to help her. I don't like feeling not in control.

The ambulance comes to a stop and at the same time, the doors open. We're greeted by a team of doctors and nurses who help unload her stretcher from the vehicle. They run through the doors, pushing me out of the way. I try to follow and not lose sight of her, but a nurse stops me.

"Please, I need to be with my wife. I need you to save her!"

She puts her hand on my chest. "Sir, I need you to calm down. You need medical attention too. You can't help your wife if you're injured. I promise that her team is doing everything they can. Come with me."

Resigning myself to getting treated, I huff, "Yes, ma'am."

Bringing me to an exam room in the emergency room, she points to the large cut on my right arm. I didn't realize how long it was since I was so focused on taking care of Mariah.

"Sit on the bed. A doctor will be by in a minute to stitch you up."

I listen only because she's right, I need to be ready to help Mariah, and because she reminds me of Irina, meaning she'd likely kick my ass if I tried to leave. It doesn't stop me from starting a return to my panicked state from the ambulance ride over here.

The doctor comes in with a suture kit on a little table on wheels. As he stitches and bandages my arm, he informs me, "I have an update on your wife. She's currently in surgery and she'll be there for a while. Someone will come to give you updates."

The nurse walks in to help the doctor clean up and she hands me a scrub top to replace my shirt, which is covered in Mariah's blood, probably mixed with some of my own. I throw it on and ask her if there's a phone I can use. "I need to call my family."

"No need, they're all in the waiting room. It's down the hall to the left."

"Thank you both so much. I appreciate it."

"Our pleasure. Best of luck to you."

I head towards where the nurse told me the waiting room was. I walk down a white hallway that opens ahead on my left to a grim looking waiting area. The chairs are gray, the tiles and walls are white. It's sterile, no emotion but numbness.

When I see my family, the room feels warmer somehow. I see my parents, plus Dima and Toly. Everyone comes to meet me halfway as I walk closer. My mom has her arms around my waist and I feel some comfort from seeing them all here.

"I grabbed your phone." Toly tosses it my way.

My mom asks how Mariah is. I just shake my head. I can feel tears coming to my eyes and I try to blink them away. "She's in surgery."

My dad gives me another hug and I tell them what the paramedic said in the ambulance. "They said something about a possible collapsed lung, and I know she had a pretty nasty gash from a piece of glass in her stomach."

Recounting her injury and remembering how quiet she was while waiting for the police to arrive, I finally break down. Dima and my dad catch me before I land on the floor and patiently help me sit down in one of the plain gray chairs.

Dima looks around for a staff member but doesn't see anyone coming. "I'll go check and see if I can find out anything new. I have privileges at this hospital." As he goes in search of an update, more of my family arrive.

Misha tells me that on his way over, he called Mariah's family to come to the hospital and told them what had happened. "Niko, as a heads-up, they brought Sylvia here. She is under arrest at the moment for a DUI charge, but the detectives at the scene assured me that they will call the ADA personally to pursue attempted murder charges and open a broader investigation into everything that's been happening."

I can't even speak, so I just nod. He continues giving me updates. "I called the ADA myself as well, on the way over. I set up a meeting for the day after tomorrow."

Everyone sits down and gets as comfortable as we can in the lobby area. In walks Mariah's family. They greet me and ask for an update. Thankfully, my dad and Misha handle that. I'm not sure if I would be able to get through it.

The three of them join us while we wait for Mariah to get out of surgery. After a few more hours of waiting, Dima gets up to go see if he can find out anything new. As he's walking to the doorway, a doctor comes around the corner and shakes Dima's hand.

"I have some good news. The surgery was successful. They're bringing Mrs. Fedorov to a room now. A nurse will come by shortly to escort two people to see her. Only two people at a time. She needs rest."

I take my first real deep breath since we got in the accident. "Thank you, Doctor. Thank you so much." I shake his hand and turn back to our families. My mom and Camila both come over to give me hugs. Very quickly, it's decided that Felipe and I will be the ones to go back when it's time.

Everyone else gets ready to leave, with promises to come back tomorrow to visit. I'm so grateful for everyone coming to make sure she's okay. Soon, it's just me and Felipe waiting to be escorted back.

The nurse coming to get us has me appreciative about finally being on my way to see my wife. I prepare myself to deal with her in bed, covered in tubes and bruises, but what greets me when we finally get to her is worse than I imagined. I'm not strong enough to see her look so fragile. She looks so pale.

I carefully and gently lean down and kiss her forehead. Felipe lifts her hand and gives it a kiss. I hear him whisper, "I love you, mija."

We drag a couple of chairs from the hallway into the room and sit for a while. "Sylvia will pay for this, Felipe. I promise you that."

"I have no doubts you'll handle it as you see fit."

"Can you think of any reason that Sylvia would've gone after Mariah like this?"

He shakes his head. "I have no clue. While we were together, she was always flaky. I always had theories that she might've had some undiagnosed mental health issues. She was incredibly paranoid and loved going to clubs. She also routinely drank heavily.

"I think my biggest regret is that I didn't search harder for Sylvia after she disappeared. I hate her for taking away my daughter, for keeping her from me her entire life." He hits his chest. "I could've raised her. She could've grown up with Juan and Bianca. She could've had a real childhood. Sylvia took away my chance to be a real father to Mariah. That's unforgiveable."

"I know that Mariah has loved getting to know you, Camila, and Juan. She's really enjoys being a big sister."

Felipe lets out a brief laugh. "Juan acts like he's her older brother."

I respond with a laugh of my own, but we both jump up out of our chairs as Mariah says, "He's protective."

Thank fuck. She's awake.

CHAPTER 27

MARIAH

I start to feel my body waking up, and I can hear Niko talking to my dad. Not opening my eyes yet, I just listen for a moment. I can feel how dry my throat is, and my whole body feels like it's been through a cheese grater.

I remember the accident and waiting for the ambulance to arrive, but it's what happened after that I'm struggling to remember. I slowly open my eyes and tell them that Juan's protective after hearing their entire conversation. Both of them jump up from their chairs to stand on either side of the bed.

"Can I have a sip of water?" I hoarsely ask, and Niko hands me a cup with a straw. I take a few sips and my dad says he'll go let the nurses know I woke up.

Niko looks really rough. He's wearing a scrub top with his suit pants. He puts his hand gently on my cheek. "How are you feeling?"

"Sore. Really sore. What happened? Did I hallucinate that my mom was the one who hit us?"

He winces. "No, I'm sorry, you didn't. It was Sylvia. She's currently in police custody after she was released from the hospital about an hour ago for some cuts and bruises she got in the accident."

I just shake my head and look up at my husband. "Why? Why does she want to hurt me? I haven't spoken to her since she left."

"We don't have a motive yet. We have two detectives on our payroll in charge of her case, they'll interview her tomorrow morning with her public defender."

There's a knock at the door of my hospital room and in walks my dad with a doctor, who says to me, "Good to see you awake, Mrs. Fedorov."

"Good to be awake."

"I just want to give you an update. You did well during surgery, but we'd like to keep you here for a couple of days for additional monitoring for infection. The cut to your abdomen was stitched up, but you did have some damage to your lung, which we were able to repair. Try to get some rest. I'll be back later to check on you. If you need anything, please let your nurses know."

"Thank you, Doctor." I smile, or at least I try to.

My dad comes to stand close to me again. "Mija, I'll be back later, okay? I'll bring Camila and Juan with me. I'm so glad you're okay." He kisses my cheek.

"Thank you for coming. I've never had a parent come when I needed help. I love you, Dad."

"Oh, sweetheart. I love you so much. I'll see you in a few hours, okay?" He wipes a stray tear away and shakes Niko's hand.

226

"Okay, thank you again for coming."

"I'll always come when you need me, mija." He waves as he leaves my room.

Niko looks like he's dead on his feet. "Can you get in bed with me?" I ask.

Shaking his head, he drags a chair closer to the bed. "You had a collapsed lung, babe. I'll sit next to you, though."

"Promise? I'm feeling sleepy again."

"Of course. Get some rest. It's the middle of the night. I'll be here when you wake up." He grabs my hand and I fall asleep feeling the weight of his larger hand against my own.

I wake up and see the clock in my room says it's now almost eleven in the morning. My hand is still tightly enveloped in Niko's. He's sitting in the chair with his top half on the mattress with me. I see the bandage on his arm. I didn't realize he was hurt in the accident last night.

He must feel me shift in the bed, because he wakes up with a jolt and looks around. "Are you okay?"

I smile at him and run my hand through his hair, which is now out of its usual bun. "I'm doing okay. Still sore, but I didn't know you were hurt last night."

"Just a few stitches, it's nothing major."

A knock on the door is quickly followed by Alexandra, Tati, and Sierra walking in. My friend darts towards me and wraps her arms around me as gently as she can, but it feels so good I ignore the pain in favor of feeling the comfort of my best friend.

"I made this for you, Aunt Mariah." Alexandra hands me a gorgeous watercolor with a bouquet of morning glories.

227

"This is really beautiful. Thank you so much." I gently smile, trying to not move my head too much.

"Here, I'll hang it up on the board." Niko takes the paper and hangs it with a magnet on the board that has my patient information on it.

Tati hands Niko a bag. "Here, Uncle Niko, Sam dropped these off for you. He figured you'd want some fresh clothes. He and I met for a while this morning and handled some of the bookkeeping together. We've got it covered while you're here."

"I appreciate that. You're doing really well. Sam and I are both proud of the work you've been doing. I know you'll handle it while I'm focused on Aunt Mariah for a little while." I know she's loving the feedback. It's so obvious how badly she wants to have the approval of her father and her uncles as she learns how to become the boss.

I wonder, if I'd grown up with my dad, would I have been the heir? Honestly, I don't think I'd do a very good job. Tati is perfectly suited to eventually take over the family, just like Juan. It's a personality type, I think.

Once Niko comes back from the bathroom in a pair of jeans and a sweater, he looks much more like his usual confident self.

Sierra hands over a cooler. "Irina packed you both some lunch. She said that hospital food is the same as prison food and not to eat it."

After they hand over everything they brought, we eat lunch and talk about anything but the accident last night. It feels good to have something normal to do, taking my mind off of the inevitable—dealing with Sylvia.

After we visit for an hour or so, my nurse comes to check on me and tells us that the detectives are here.

"We'll leave you to talk to them. Say goodbye, girls." Sierra ushers them out after they carefully give me hugs.

Niko looks concerned. "Are you sure that you're up for this? We can tell them to come back later."

"I'll be fine. I'd rather do it now than put it off any longer."

He goes out to the hallway, then escorts the two male detectives into the room.

"Hello, Mrs. Fedorov. My name is Detective Baker. This is my colleague, Detective Nelson. We're here to talk to you about Sylvia Perez. In addition to the accident that occurred last night, we've received information that she was harassing you?"

"I would argue that she was stalking me. I've been receiving calls and letters, and I was attacked last week by a man who was paid with drugs by Sylvia to hurt me." I continue to tell them the entire story.

Once I'm done, Niko adds, "I can have the notes that were left on her door, along with pictures of her apartment that was ransacked, brought to the station."

Detective Nelson confirms they want that evidence. "We'd appreciate that. Thank you, Mr. Fedorov."

Niko asks them both, "Is there any update, or anything you can tell us?"

Detective Baker answers this time. "She was questioned this morning with a public defender present. Now that we've spoken to you, we will want to talk to her again. She's currently being held without bond. The ADA will likely pursue a slew of charges, considering how much evidence you have." He looks at Niko. "Anatoly Fedorov forwarded CCTV footage and surveillance images with timestamps. That should expedite the investigation."

"It's good to hear my brother-in-law already sent the footage. Did Sylvia mention what the motive was? Did you learn why she wanted to hurt me?" I just want to know why so badly.

Baker looks sympathetic when he tells me, "No, ma'am. I'm sorry, a motive hasn't been established yet."

Nelson wraps up their visit though, when he says, "We'll get out of your hair and let you rest. We may need some additional information from you, but we'll give you a call if it's necessary. If you have any questions for us, please don't hesitate to reach out. We'll keep you in the loop with everything, though."

I nod, grateful they kept this short and concise. "Thank you, both. Appreciate the update, and you listening to everything I had to share."

Once they leave, I pout at Niko.

"Why are you looking like that?" He laughs, knowing I don't usually make puppy dog eyes at him.

"Well, I think that out of everything, I'm mostly pissed that Sylvia is the reason we aren't going to Rapture tonight."

He shakes his head. "Babe, you're literally in a hospital bed recovering from a collapsed lung and a long surgery."

"I know, but I miss having sex. It's your fault, really, you turned me into a nympho."

"My poor baby. As soon as you're cleared by the doctors, I'll happily fuck you into the mattress."

I can't help the goose bumps that rush up my arms thinking about Niko getting rougher with me. We never got much further than introductory sex during our initial portion of my contract with him, before we got married. And since then, we've had sex a few times, but we never got to take it to the next level. I'm desperate for it if I'm being honest.

He sees the effect his words are having on me, so he continues his dirty talking tease. "I'll show everyone how good my wife is. How well she submits to me. I'll edge you for hours before I finally give you my cock."

"Is that supposed to scare me?"

"Not at all." He turns serious before he continues. "I scheduled my vasectomy while you slept this morning. It'll be perfect timing—we can recover together."

I'm too scared to believe that I really found a man who's willing to be child-free. "Are you sure?"

"I'm positive. I don't want children, I want you. We can be the fun aunt and uncle. We can sneak them extra cookies and be the place they run away to when they're eventually mad at their parents.

"But most importantly, I want to bear the brunt of making sure we prevent pregnancy. You can continue taking birth control if you want, but know that you won't need to."

This man is too perfect. "I love you. Niko, I don't know what I did to deserve you, but I'm so happy you volunteered to marry me."

He shakes his head. "Did you think I was going to let someone else have you? Good one."

"Can I have a kiss?"

He walks closer to me and leans down, putting his lips on mine. I can taste a different toothpaste on his tongue from the hospital bathroom. But the feeling I get when we're connected? It's like coming home.

Over the next few days, I have a constant rotation of visitors. Everyone in the Fedorov family, my own family, even Ilya and Irina stop by.

I meet the benchmarks to be discharged on the fifth day, and I'm so fucking happy to be going home to climb into my own bed.

Dima and Sierra alternate my home care. They also help Niko when he gets his vasectomy the day after I'm home. With both of us recovering, he lets me introduce him to *Modern Family,* and we binge the entire series.

I took a leave of absence from work to recover. My company was very understanding, and my boss offered me paid leave once the story of what my mom did broke in the news. I've been bored though, so I've offered to help Niko do some admin stuff, but I know he won't let me work too hard.

As I lie in bed next to him, I smile at how good my life really is, crazy mom aside.

Chapter 28

Niko

Two Weeks Later

I wake up and see Mariah's still asleep next to me, but my phone is buzzing on the nightstand. I open my phone, and the notifications tell me that the group chat is popping off.

> Toly: We've got intel that there's a trafficking shipment coming through the ports to rails headed to Mexico.

> Vlad: Any dates on that yet?

> Misha: Should we loop in Alvarez?

> Toly: Vlad, not yet. Misha, probably. They control the ports in Indiana, so it'd be easier to have them all on lock down.

> Misha: Copy. I'll give them a call later today.

> Misha: Oh, Niko, when you read this call me. The ADA told me Sylvia is pleading guilty. Sentencing will be in February.

I ignore all the messages and just call Misha.

"Hey, Niko. You see the messages?"

"Yeah, but I'm focused on the part where you mentioned Sylvia."

"She's facing twenty years. With all the charges, it's likely she'll get at least fifteen with the guilty plea."

"Not enough. She should rot in there for what she's done to Mariah her entire life."

"I agree, which is why the ADA offered me an off-the-books favor."

"Which is?"

"If Mariah would like to meet with Sylvia, without it being on record, to get some answers and closure, there's a window of two hours that the ADA will have her moved out of the housing unit. You'll need to be there at one o'clock today."

I don't need to wake Mariah to know that she'll want to go. "We'll be there. Thank you for this. She needs to face her mom. Even if she doesn't get answers, she needs to say some things."

"I figured as much. I hope she gets what she needs."

"Me too. I'll talk to you later. Thanks for setting this up."

I lay my phone back on the bedside table and roll over to spoon Mariah. I hold her in my arms, grateful she survived everything her mother threw her way. I'm so fucking proud of her.

I hold her and keep her close, letting her sleep for a while longer. I feel the moment she wakes up, because she moves her ass against my cock. "Careful, baby. We have somewhere to be later."

"Where's that?"

"Misha called. He arranged with the district attorney to get you an off-the-record visit with Sylvia." I refuse to call that woman her mother. She abused my wife, she doesn't get that title. She doesn't deserve it.

"Yes, please. I want to go. Even if she doesn't tell me why, I want to be able to look her in the eye and know that I made it out. I did all of this despite the way she treated me. It'll be good for me to close this chapter of my life."

She's been seeing a therapist a couple of times per week since the car wreck to work through some of the trauma. She said that the therapist she's seeing is the same one she saw in the wake of Sierra's parents' deaths. I'm glad she's getting the help she needs.

I wish I could be the one to offer her everything necessary to help her get past this, but I know that's selfish and unrealistic.

It's getting close to ten a.m., so I need to throw on some workout clothes so I can meet Toly in the gym. "Mind if I work out with my brother?"

"No, of course not. I'm going to take a long bath. I can have an early lunch waiting for you when you get back, then we can head over to the jail?"

"Yeah, that should work. I'll see you in a while." I jump out of bed and readjust my bun before putting on a pair of shorts and a t-shirt. Toly's waiting for me near the elevator, and we have a long lifting session. I'm glad we had this planned so I can take out some of my anger at Sylvia in a healthier way before seeing her in person.

After I eat lunch with Mariah, I jump in the shower to clean up after my workout. Half an hour before the scheduled meeting, we head down to the garage. My new SUV is parked in one of the closer spots. We climb in and head over to the Cook County Jail.

Walking in, Mariah reaches for my hand as we go through security. ADA Sweeney is there waiting for us. I've seen her before, in passing, at different political events over the years. She's gaining a reputation

235

for being a fair ADA, hopefully she continues down that path. Many in the DA's office will decline to prosecute if they deem it too hard a case, but Sweeney is said to never back down when the evidence is there.

"You'll have about an hour. I thought I could squeeze them for two, but the warden is in a mood today," she explains the slight change in plans.

"No worries. Thank you for helping make this happen, miss." Sierra reaches back for my hand as we walk into an empty office with just a desk and a few chairs. The three of us sit down and see the woman who birthed Mariah up close for the first time. She's sat across from us, by the correctional officers, still handcuffed. Mariah is visibly shaken, but I can tell she's also trying to muster up the strength to portray indifference to Sylvia.

"Why did you do it, Sylvia?" Mariah looks directly at the woman sitting cuffed to the table.

The woman is clearly still dealing with some withdrawal symptoms from whatever she was hooked on, but she's coherent enough for this conversation.

Instead of acting like a grown woman, Sylvia sneers at Mariah. "You had no right to go and figure out who your father was. I knew he was cheating on me because he'd leave at all hours of the night without warning. Did you know that? He'd be unreachable for days at a time. I kept you a secret to punish him."

He wasn't cheating. It's clear that Sylvia didn't know at the time that Felipe is the leader of a cartel. He was probably fixing problems or taking care of shipments, definitely not cheating. He's too good of a man to do something like that. Even if he didn't want to marry

236

a woman, he'd never cheat. That's considered dishonorable in our world.

Mariah knows she's not going to get a better answer from Sylvia on this topic, so she moves on to a different subject. "Why did you leave me like you did? I was still a kid."

This woman laughs at Mariah. "You know why. You're a slut. You wanted all of my boyfriends. I know the way they'd look at you the minute you grew tits, so I made you someone else's problem. I figured you'd just end up in foster care." Sylvia just shrugs her shoulders, like abandoning her daughter was the obvious choice.

I'm done listening to this woman spew shit at my wife. I clench my jaw, knowing that this is for Mariah. She needs this, so I choose to give Sylvia a warning. "Watch it."

Mariah moves to a third question. "Why the stalking? How'd you even find out about the DNA test?"

Sylvia once again laughs in Mariah's face, like this is all just a joke to her. "I was arrested on a prostitution charge. My customer was an undercover cop. But while I was inside, I was bunking with a cartel mule who said that someone high up found out they have a sister. That's when I learned my whore of a daughter was trying to get her hands on some money that really should've been mine for raising you as long as I did. If I couldn't have Felipe, you sure as fuck weren't going to have him."

This woman's off her rocker. Somehow this mule knew back in early fall that Juan had found Mariah, and this crazy bitch immediately knew she was talking about the daughter she left behind? What are the chances?

"So who were the men who kept calling me?"

"Just random johns. I'd have them make a call after I finished them off. I wanted you to be so scared you wouldn't leave your house."

I'm floored. This really all started because of the delusions of a drug addict who likely also has some untreated mental health issues. She chose to hurt her daughter, to try and kill her own child. For her entire life, Sylvia chose herself over Mariah.

I put my hand on Mariah's leg for support, but I can no longer stay silent. "Not only does Mariah have the full force of the Alvarez Cartel behind her, but as the wife of a senior member of the Fedorov Bratva, Mariah is more than just protected. She's a queen."

My words must give Mariah some of her confidence back, because she tells Sylvia, "I hope you live out your days in agony, like you deserve."

She gets up and doesn't give Sylvia another glance. We walk out of the room and I thank ADA Sweeney again for allowing this visit.

Once we leave the jail, we head home, where Dima meets us and takes another look at Mariah's wounds. The stitches have dissolved, and he gives her the go-ahead for exercise. Nothing too intense, but she should be good.

Fucking finally. We've been aching for each other. I've been limited to eating her out for the past few days, and I finally just felt good enough after my vasectomy a few days ago. I can fuck my wife again.

After my cousin leaves, I know I'll have to follow him in a few minutes for an all-hands meeting at Misha's. Before I leave, I ask her, "Would you want to go to Rapture tomorrow?"

Her eyes light up, and she enthusiastically says yes.

"I'll reserve a room for us, then. I also have to go to that meeting with everyone. I told you that my family and yours have worked together before on things like this, and tonight is one of those times."

I told her that we have information on a possible rescue mission. I could tell she was nervous, she knows that there is a risk of us getting injured during these, but it's something we all believe in.

I go and get ready. When I come back into the living room, she's already under a blanket with her latest book. I give her a kiss, and she looks to me as I walk out. "Please be safe and come home to me."

"Always. I love you."

"Love you too. Go kill some traffickers and save some people."

"That's the plan, baby."

Chapter 29

Niko

A s much as I didn't want to leave Mariah tonight, especially after she was finally cleared for some physical activity, I arrive at my brother's house. Dima is getting out of his own car. We give each other a nod, despite just having seen each other.

There are also about a dozen Alvarez soldiers hanging out with some of our own guards. Headlights come into view from the bottom of the driveway, and I see it's Sam. He parks his car next to mine, greeting me and Dima.

Normally, when we do a large-scale rescue operation like this, we just all pile into the large family room. When I walk in, I see that we're some of the last to arrive. I see my own family, including Tati. My in-laws are also sitting among the Fedorov men. Felipe comes over and says hello, asking about Mariah.

I smile because my wife really does deserve to have a parent worry and love her like Felipe does. "She's doing well. She probably already was talking to Camila about this, but we'd love to have you all over next weekend to celebrate her birthday."

His face brightens when he smiles. "We'd love to be there! I'm sure my wife's already on top of it. I appreciate everything you do for Mariah."

"I'll always take care of my wife, she's amazing."

"You'll get no argument from me. My daughter is a gift."

We rejoin the rest of the men when I hear Toly whistle loud enough to wake the dead. He hands over the meeting to Misha and Vlad.

Vlad clears his throat before giving us background on what the plan is for tonight. "Earlier this week, we received a tip from a former Kuznetsov informant in New York, who is now with the family we installed in that territory, that one of Sergei's old contacts was trying to move a boatload of people through the Great Lakes before putting them on trains headed south to Mexico and Central America."

This right here is where formalizing this alliance comes to fruition. Neither organization stands for human trafficking or even involving innocent people at all in our operations. We also each bring different expertise to the table. My family's weapons are so much better that even the Alvarezes buy from us, and their foot soldiers have always been able to gain intel even our top guys can't.

Juan continues explaining the rescue plans. "We plan to meet the boat at the docks and intercept the victims before they can be loaded onto the train. This will give us the best chance to get them to safety while also catching the bastards on the boat and the ones handling the exchange at the train yard on the edge of the dock's property."

Misha wraps up the meeting by giving everyone their placements and mission roles. We break apart to get prepped to roll out. I go to the armory to grab weapons and a Kevlar vest. Tati hands me a leg holster before grabbing one for herself. At almost fourteen, she is growing up so fast, but she's been training for about a year now and is ready for her first mission like this one. She was a part of the rescue of Sierra and Vlad earlier in the summer, but this is a planned assault. It'll be a good test for her, since she wants to be trusted with more responsibility.

I'll be keeping a close eye on her during this mission. When we go in and rescue these men, women, and sometimes children, they can look really rough. They have been through hell and back during their time being held by these scumbags. It can be a lot to see, even for me.

As we walk out to the SUVs, everyone grabs a radio and headset. We move over to the docks in a convoy, and as we park out of sight, Toly comes over the radio. "The boat we're after is about forty-five minutes from arrival. We'll have just enough time to get into position."

"Copy."

Looking around, I see soldiers moving quietly to get in position. I find my own spot. When Toly comes back over the radio thirty-five minutes later, he lets everyone know "We have company. The people handling train transport have arrived to help tie the boat to the dock."

Nobody dares to respond, but it's getting difficult to stay still as we start to see men and women ranging in ages from what look like teenagers to late-twenties. Some are in better shape than others, but all of them need to get off the boat before we can make our move.

From my vantage spot, I can see Juan dropping the explosives onto the boat's bow. Once he's a safe distance away from the boat, Misha comes over the radio, giving the signal for everyone to move in.

Toly and I head for the victims, along with Tati and a handful of soldiers. Dima starts to pick off the traffickers one by one from his sniper's perch, allowing our other tactical teams more of an advantage when trying to capture the rest of them alive.

I look over at Toly. He's got a strange look on his face. His behavior is off as we make our way over to the victims, who are now huddling together, trying to stay warm in the chilly January temperatures. None of them are dressed for the below-freezing Chicago weather.

Glancing back at my brother again, I see his eyes are now focused on one of the victims in particular. She appears to be in her early to midtwenties. But she's been pulled away from the other victims by one of the traffickers. He's using her as a shield now, holding a gun to her head.

The other victims are being led to waiting vans by Tati and our soldiers, so I choose to go help Toly as he starts to chase after the young woman and her kidnapper. Her eyes are pleading with us to save her.

Toly points his gun at the scumbag. "Let her go!"

"Not happening." And he keeps his gun to her temple. The woman is trying to wiggle free and fight back, but she's obviously been beaten, even looks malnourished. I can see Toly in my peripheral vision, and he's starting to look distraught.

The kidnapper forces the woman into a car, and I'm forced to hold Toly back from trying to chase after them. He's fighting with me to break free, but I make him a promise. "We'll get her back, okay? We will find her."

He looks in my eyes, almost manically. "I will get her back. I'll do whatever it takes to find her. I got the license plate, not that it matters. Those sick fucks probably stole their vehicles."

I pull him in for a hug. I don't know what sort of connection he felt to this woman, but I can see it's affecting him. "Come on, let's help the rest of the team."

We walk back to the group and everyone's split into two teams, one working with Dima on doing initial treatment on the victims and the other restraining and loading the traffickers into vans to go back to the basement.

We'll try to get intel out of them before we dispose of them. People who traffic other people don't deserve redemption. Toly turns to me as we approach everyone else. "I'm going to go to the basement. I need to know who the one man was so that I can get my angel back."

I know he still struggles with these rescues after his own rescue over fifteen years ago. I was in high school when it happened, and he's never told anyone everything that he endured. We've all tried to talk to him. Our parents even had one of the wives of a ranking member speak with Toly. She was a therapist, and while I think it helped a little, he's buried a lot of it.

This is the first time in at least thirty rescue missions he's ever responded that way to a victim we weren't able to save. I can't help but wonder if that means something. I'll do whatever I can to help him find her.

Tati is getting all the victims' information so that we can contact families for those who want to go home, or get them set up with new identities if they'd rather move on from whatever situations they've left behind.

244

Soldiers help them get into the remaining vans to drive back to my building. We keep two floors of apartments directly below Toly's and my penthouses vacant. After making a few trips in the elevators, we get them all settled.

There are plenty of beds for them, and all the bathrooms are fully stocked. We also try to keep new packages of underwear and basic sweat suits so they can change out of whatever clothes they were wearing. Tati is helping show some of the women around the kitchen of the larger apartment. She did really well tonight.

I should go downstairs to check in on our newest residents of the basement interrogation rooms, but right now I just want to go home to my wife. I jump in the elevator, and when I walk in my front door, Mariah is waiting for me in the same place I left her earlier this afternoon. She's changed into some comfy pajamas, but she looks so beautiful.

"You're home!" She smiles at me and comes to greet me with a kiss.

"I'm home."

"How'd it go?"

"I'll tell you while we get ready for bed. I'm exhausted."

I change into a pair of sweats and take off my glasses. I climb into bed next to Mariah and pull her to me so her head is lying on my bare chest. I tell her everything that happened, including Toly being strange about the one woman. I assure her that I'll help him find her.

"I'm proud of you all. I love you, Nikolai."

"I love you, sweetheart. I'm so glad I got to marry you. It's the best thing I've ever done." We both drift off to sleep, and the last thing I think about is how really lucky I am to have such an incredible wife.

CHAPTER 30
MARIAH

I wake up as a little spoon, with Niko at my back. I feel his cock and I move my ass so it grinds against him. It wakes him up and his moan lets me know he likes feeling me moving around. I reach behind me and put my hand down his sweatpants.

I've been feeling more daring when it comes to initiating sex, and Niko's told me that even though he's dominant, seeing me starting to feel confident is sexy. He encourages it. I would never want to be the one in control during sex—I'm more than happy to leave that to him—but letting him know I'm horny isn't a hardship.

"Let me make you cum, wife."

I roll over so I'm on my back, and his warm hand reaches into my pajama shorts. His fingers touch near my entrance, feeling how wet I am for him. He uses some of it as lube to glide over my clit. I arch my back at how good it feels to have him slowly, but with pressure, touch my clit. His lips find mine as he continues to play with my pussy. I use my hand to try and get his pants down enough to release his cock. Luckily, he notices and helps me out. Once I can fully stroke his dick, we slowly work each other up to orgasm. The release feels so good, but nothing will ever replace the feeling of him inside me. I can't wait to go back to Rapture tonight.

We lie there for a minute, catching our breaths, before I ask if he's heard from Toly after last night.

"I haven't yet, but I'm sure that he's stayed up all night trying to track her. Let's go make some breakfast."

We eat and get ready for the day. Even though we'll be going to Rapture later tonight, we have separate plans for today. I will be going with Camila to shop for some baby things that are on Sierra's registry for her baby shower.

I have to wait for Ilya to get here since he's been transferred to be my personal guard. Niko told me during breakfast that while it might sound like a demotion, being trusted to guard the Pakhan's family is the highest honor.

I'm grabbing my purse when there's a knock on the front door, and when I open it, Tati is there, along with Ilya. "Hi, you guys. Come on in."

Niko comes over to tell me that he and Tati will be working on inventory for the strip clubs and he will be showing her some of the real estate portfolio for Fedorov Industries.

"I used to think this stuff would be boring, but it's actually super cool. It's more tech based than I thought, which I really like after spending most of last year working with Uncle Toly," she informs me, and Niko tries to hide a smile.

I can't believe she's almost fourteen. Our birthdays are only two days apart, and we'll be celebrating with the whole family. We also share a favorite food, Irina's beef stroganoff, so we both are excited for the following weekend's party.

"Alright, you two, have fun. Ilya and I will be shopping for baby Kira!" I turn to walk out the door and Ilya leads me to an SUV.

"So, Niko tells me you're my guard now?"

"Yeah, I was told last night that the Pakhan wanted me to be your full-time guard. It's an honor. I can't believe they trust me. It's a lot of responsibility, but I promise, Sierra, I'll protect you with my life."

"Let's hope it never comes to that, but since I need a bodyguard, I'm glad it's you." I smile at him in the rearview mirror. We meet Camila for lunch at a Thai restaurant in the same plaza as the baby store. Her guard and Ilya sit at the table next to ours and we enjoy a great lunch. It's been fun getting to know her outside of my dad and Juan. She is such a kind woman. When I was in the hospital, she kept me company. We got to have some substantial conversations.

We walk over to the large baby store, and I'm able to quickly find the bedding on Sierra's registry. I also can't stop myself when I see some cute headbands and onesies. Camila and I talk about some of the games we're planning for the shower, and she adds a few suggestions of her own. She'll be coming to the party as well. I really appreciate that even though they weren't allies before, my family and the Fedorovs are comfortable enough to interact socially for my benefit.

When we're done shopping, Camila says goodbye before Ilya and I head back home.

"Thanks for coming with me. I'm home until Niko gets here. We have plans later."

He nods. "No worries, the normal guards are here. I'll be on call for when you have to leave home. I'll also be here during weekdays. There's no pressure—it's my job now. Text me if you have changes to scheduled plans and I'll make sure you're covered."

Once he leaves for the day, I head straight to the shower and get ready for later. The clock on my phone says I have about an hour before Niko said to be ready. I put some makeup on and do my hair in a braid. I go to the closet where a small bag is hidden under some old boots. Inside is a sexy set of lingerie I picked up a couple of days ago. The red pops against my skin tone, and I know that Niko goes feral when I wear red. It reminds him of our first night together, before he freaked out.

Looking in the mirror, I can see the scars I have from the accident. I don't necessarily feel self-conscious, but I hate that my mom was able to do so much damage. I shake off the slight tingle of insecurity, and pull off a dress from the hanger that is the same shade of red as my lingerie. It's a somewhat tight dress that accentuates my figure.

As I'm zipping the dress, Niko walks into the closet. "Fuck, you look amazing. So goddamn beautiful, babe. Are you ready to go?"

"You look good yourself." He's wearing a black suit with a black button-down shirt. His hair is down and looks freshly washed, still a little wet.

Explaining his hair, he says, "I got ready in the guest room. Tati and I ran a little longer than I realized. I didn't want us to be late or interrupt your time in here."

"Well, let's go, husband. I'm excited to go back."

We walk hand in hand to his Porsche and make the short drive to River North. We're greeted by Iris in the lobby, and as we walk towards the playroom, Niko pulls me aside. "Do I have your permission to be your dom tonight?"

"Yes, sir. Please." I'm so excited because I really like being in this dynamic with him. We only had a few times together before everything blew up.

As we enter the large open room, I see Sam. He greets us with "Hello. Enjoy your evening, you two" and a wink as he passes by with two gorgeous women, heading towards the private rooms.

"Are you sure about this? I'm going to let everyone see how beautiful my wife is when she submits to me."

I clench my thighs together. I want him to show me off, to be proud that I'm his wife. I can feel my panties getting drenched from how turned on I am.

"Don't worry, sweetheart, I'll be the only one to ever touch you."

Niko didn't need to tell me that. I know he'd never let another man or woman touch me. I belong to him, just how I like it.

He reaches to unzip the top half of my dress. He groans when he sees the balconette style bra I'm wearing. I can tell he's rock hard as he puts his hand on my shoulder, gently pushing me to my knees. A crowd starts to form around us as he nods to me, giving me permission to take out his cock. I reach for the zipper of his pants and pull them and his boxer briefs down so I can release his dick.

He's already dripping precum as I lean forward to lick the tip of his engorged cock. I start to bob my head up and down, gagging when he hits the back of my throat. I can feel more eyes on me as I begin to gag louder. Niko's fucking my face now, and I wrap my hands around his muscular thighs, taking it all.

As he pulls back to take his cock out of my mouth, I hear groans of frustration from our spectators. I look up at Niko, who just says, "I'm only going to cum in that tight pussy of yours."

I decide to be a brat and suck him back into my mouth. I use both of my hands plus my mouth. I start to twist my hands in opposite directions and I don't let up until I feel him cum down my throat.

He laughs and says to our crowd, "Should my sub get punished for disobeying her dom like that?"

Everyone nods, and I hear a few cheers for Niko to give me a punishment. If I could, I'd cheer too. I've never gotten a real punishment yet, and I know that he can't go too hard because of my injuries, but I'm sure he'll make it worth my while to disobey.

"Color?"

"Green."

"Good girl. Bend over." I see him holding a flogger. I have no clue how it got into his hands, but the anticipation has me teetering on the edge. He takes my dress fully off now, leaving me in my bra, underwear, and heels.

I bend over into position and feel his hand on my lower back, "Mariah, you need to use your safe-words if necessary. Your injuries are still relatively fresh."

"I know, and I will if I need them."

"I will give you ten—five on each side." He starts with no warning, and I feel the burn on my ass and upper thighs. When he's done I start to beg him to let me cum. He doesn't answer me, but helps me up and leads me to one of the private rooms. He throws me down on a bed before he strips out of his clothes. I watch him slowly get naked in front of me. His body is incredible. Every ridge of muscle has desire running rampant through my veins.

Niko stalks over to the bed and that's when I notice the bed is equipped with restraints. He takes each of my arms and puts the cuffs around my wrists before he finally crawls onto the bed between my legs. "Fuck, Mariah. I can see how wet your pussy is. Those pretty red panties are soaked."

He takes off my underwear and notches himself against me. Soon, he sets a deep, unforgiving rhythm.

"You're such a good sub, even when you're being a brat. I'm so fucking obsessed with you."

I can feel the moment he cums inside me. It forces me over the edge, and I experience an intense orgasm of my own. He stays inside me for a moment, letting me feel the connection of him and me being one. He carefully pulls out of me. While he's still on top, he releases my wrists and kisses each one after it's freed from the cuffs.

Even though he got his vasectomy, there's still more follow-up to make sure he's good to go, so I've still been taking my birth control. I can't wait to do all of this without worrying. It'll be a big relief; one I'm so grateful for.

"I can't believe we started off here only two months ago."

He winces. "I'm so sorry again for how I acted on that first night. I hate myself for the way I left you."

I put my hand on his chest. "Niko, you more than groveled and have made up for that. You've apologized, and I've forgiven you. I mean, you married me to keep me safe."

He laughs. "Yeah, well, I saw the opportunity to get my dream girl. I wasn't about to let you slip through my fingers."

Epilogue

Mariah - Five Months Later

T hings have settled down since everything that happened during the holidays. My mom did eventually enter a guilty plea and was sentenced back in February. She's currently serving her fifteen years at a prison in southern Illinois.

After we celebrated my twenty-ninth birthday, Niko told me that he'd like to give me a proper wedding. I tried to tell him that our first wedding was special and that everyone was there for that one. He was insistent, saying, "You deserve to plan the wedding of your dreams with more than three hours' notice. Plus, your family didn't get to be there."

And that last point is what had me giving in. It's also how the entire Fedorov and Alvarez families ended up on a large private jet heading to the Fedorov family's private island in the Caribbean.

It took a lot of planning to make sure both organizations were covered as all the leaders were essentially on vacation, but everyone made it happen.

I'm sitting with Kira, who is just a couple of months old. I can see Niko playing cards with both of our other nieces. His eyes meet mine and I smile. We love having such great kids in our lives, but we've been able to travel and do our own thing these past few months.

My dad comes and sits down next to me. I asked Camila to send him my way once they finished lunch.

"I was told you were looking for me, mija?"

"At our first wedding, Maxim was kind enough to walk me down the aisle. Even though we'd met, it had only been earlier that day. The last six months have been incredible, and I'm so happy you're all in my life.

"I've been fully accepted as an Alvarez, and I'd really love it if you would walk me down the aisle this time."

I can see his eyes welling up with tears.

"I'd be honored."

He kisses my cheek, careful not to disturb Kira as she enjoys her milk coma.

The plane lands a little while later, and we arrive at the villa. It's large enough to host everyone, even my family. Misha and Sierra are such gracious hosts. We enjoy the first few days on the boats, in the water, lying out in the sun, and just relaxing.

***

I'm woken up by Niko telling me that all the women are waiting for me, along with a full glam team. I walk out to the kitchen in search of coffee, but I'm met with Anastasia and Camila fawning over me. I love that I have these two in my life. They're both amazing women who've raised such great men.

Sierra, Tati, Alexandra, and Irina join us as we enjoy some pastries with our coffee, and milk for the girls. We all coo over Kira, who's recently learned how to giggle. It's so cute. She's such a smart baby at eleven weeks old.

The hair and makeup artists start to set up different stations so they can manage getting seven women ready. For the next couple of hours, we enjoy mimosas as our hair is styled perfectly and makeup applied flawlessly. The team Sierra hired is the real deal.

Keeping me on schedule, Sierra tells me it's time to get dressed. I did end up buying a dress this time because I didn't want Anastasia's to get ruined at the beach. I was able to find a flowy dress that has a tight bodice and a loose skirt. It's strapless, with a slight embroidery detail around the edges. Understated, but really pretty for the setting and it suits my own personal style.

The rest of the women have left to put on their own dresses when I hear a knock on the door. Opening it, I see my dad and Maxim waiting in the hallway. I usher them inside, and they both tell me how beautiful I look.

Maxim is so gracious. He was so glad to hear that I asked my dad to walk me down the aisle. "I'm so happy you and Nikolai found each other. I love seeing my son filled with so much passion and being such a good husband."

My dad nods. "Yeah, and your son better know how amazing my daughter is or I'll have to send her brother to remind him."

We all laugh. Juan's become protective of me, which is funny to see when he and Niko are worried about me together. They team up and try to wrap me in a bubble. Niko just likes having an ally in defending me. I know I'm in trouble when Ilya's also around. The three of them together are quite funny.

"I'll go make sure my son is ready. Again, you look stunning, Mariah." After kissing my cheek, Maxim heads off in search of Niko, leaving me and my dad alone.

He hands me a small velvet bag. I open it and inside is a beautiful bracelet with rubies all around it. "These should match the ones I gave you at Christmas. I had it made for you—a gift for your wedding day."

"It's beautiful. Can you help me put it on?"

He puts the jewels around my wrist, securing the clasp. "Te amo, mija."

"Te amo, Papa."

I'm pulled into a hug, but a knock on the door from Sierra has us reaching for my bouquet on the table.

"Are you ready? Niko looks really good." She wiggles her eyebrows suggestively. I just laugh. Misha would hate to hear that she thinks Niko looks good.

The three of us walk out to the backyard area that faces the ocean, where Sam is standing next to Niko. We asked him to be the officiant for the vow renewal. He was more than happy, and has been working on the ceremony for the past month.

With my arm in my dad's, I walk down the aisle to my husband, whose eyes are just as misty as my own. Sam's version of a wedding ceremony is heartfelt and personal. He took the time to make it about Niko and me. When he tells Niko he can kiss his wife, my husband mauls me, kissing me in a way that is not at all PG.

We move to a tent that was set up for the small reception. I walk over to my dad. "Would you join me for a daddy-daughter dance?"

"Of course!" He jumps up and we share a dance, just the two of us.

Niko comes along after the song is over and we dance together, with everyone soon joining in around us. Alexandra and Niko begin to dance as another slow song plays from the speakers, so I head back to the table to sit and have a drink. I notice Toly off to the side on his own.

I sit next to him. "You okay? And I'll know if you're lying to me."

He gives me a short smile. "You're good for my brother, you know that?"

"Stop deflecting, Anatoly."

"Damn, full name?" He sighs. "I wish I could find her. It's been months and she could be really hurt. I have a lead, but I can't make that trip happen for another couple of weeks. I need to do some more recon before I make the trek."

"If you need to leave here early, you should go. I don't want her to be waiting for you longer than she has to."

Shaking his head, he tells me, "I already sent a team before we left to come here. They're gathering as much info as possible so I can hit the ground running when I go there next week."

"Is it her?"

"I think so, but my team will send a photo when they can, to get confirmation."

I put my hand on his. "You'll get her back. I know you will. This is deeply personal to you."

He tries to deny it, but I know what Niko told me that night. "You know, Toly, it's okay to fall in love. I waited almost twenty-nine years to feel it, so I know it's real. When you get her back, you need to be patient with her, show her love, and help her heal."

"We can heal each other. Congratulations again, and welcome to the family, Mariah." He finishes his drink before heading back inside the house.

Niko comes over and asks if everything's okay. I stand up to give my husband a kiss before pulling him back to the dance floor. Dima and Juan are dancing with the girls. Even my mother-in-law makes her way over to dance with us.

Misha's got Kira strapped to his chest as he sways back and forth. I get to spend a second night celebrating my marriage with everyone I love.

Later, when Niko and I are getting ready for bed, I tell Niko a secret. "You know, I never thought I would have a family again after Sierra's parents died. But today, I felt like I was surrounded by so much love and support. It was more than I ever could've dreamed of."

"I'll spend the rest of my life showing you nothing but love and devotion. You're everything I could've ever wanted. I love you so fucking much, Mariah."

"I love you. Good night, husband."

COMING SOON

Book three in the Fedorov Bratva series will be... Anatoly's book!

Title: A Phoenix For Anatoly

Release Date: May 2026

Blurb:

When Anatoly Fedorov saw a young woman being led away from him, and safety, during a rescue of trafficking victims, he resolved to do whatever it took to find her. He knew what it was like to spend time in captivity after being kidnapped as a teenager. He not only saw the fight in her eyes, but an instant and deep connection.

Valerie Walker grew up in a loving family, but the last few months have been nearly impossible to survive. After missing a chance at escape, she struggles to stay positive. She holds out hope that the man with deep brown eyes and a scar on his cheek will keep searching for her.

Their connection formed in a millisecond, but for each of them, it was undeniable. Anatoly will do anything he can to find his angel and bring her back to safety, in his arms.

Acknowledgments

Thank you to everyone who's read this book. Being an independent author, each page read matters. I hope you enjoyed Nikolai and Mariah's story as much as I did.

Michael, thank you for being a continued source of support and love for me. You're always the one I can't wait to celebrate my accomplishments with and lean on when times get difficult. Anytime I've struggled while writing, you are there to help me work through it. I'm the person I am today because of your love for the past ten years. I can't wait for another decade together and the memories we will make.

To my book-less book club, thank you for your endless support as I continue writing more books. With everything from helping choose character details to beta reading very rough first drafts, you all have been amazing. I'm so lucky to have you in my life. Anytime we're together, I know I'll laugh my ass off.

To my family, thank you again for everything you've done to encourage my reading and imagination. It's because of that support I've been able to make my dream of writing stories possible.

About the Author

I grew up reading everything from *Boxcar Children* to *Nancy Drew* books. I fell in love with reading at an early age and loved to imagine what it'd be like to write my own book one day.

As an adult, I fell back in love with reading. After having read a few hundred romance novels myself, I decided to write some of my own with the goal of writing unique plots featuring some of my favorite tropes. I want to give readers something fresh in a world of so many options.

Website: anncaroll.com

Sign-up for my newsletter: Click here

Follow me on social!

Instagram: @AnnCarollAuthor

TikTok: AnnCarollAuthor

www.ingramcontent.com/pod-product-compliance
Lightning Source LLC
Chambersburg PA
CBHW060625260626
47161CB00008B/2800